Brooklyn

I stood there with the horse, petting his velvet nose, trying to absorb his quiet calm to help ease my jangling nerves.

It worked a little, until *he* returned, striding toward the outdoor arena, looking amazingly sexy in his riding outfit. Suddenly, like he was on a mission, he walked straight up to me. His eyes burned into mine and when he didn't stop a few feet away, I began to panic.

Because I was suddenly sure he was going to grab me and kiss me.

My lungs froze on a breath. My heart began to race.

And then he stopped right in front of me, inside my bubble and close enough that I could smell him; leather, saddle soap, boy.

I looked up at him. His lips were turned up in a slight smile and then they parted. He reached up toward my face, his eyes taking me in with his usual intensity. My cheeks flushed, but ached for his touch. I licked my dry lips and swallowed, suddenly worried about too much saliva. I did not want to ruin this kiss. My eyes fluttered closed as he leaned in.

Taking the Reins

The Rosewoods, Book 1

by

Katrina Abbott

Over The Cliff Publishing, 2014

This is a work of fiction. Similarities to real people, places or events are entirely coincidental.

TAKING THE REINS

Second edition. June 1, 2016

ISBN-13: 978-1533558459
ISBN-10: 1533558450

10 9 8 7 6 5 4 3

For Steven,
who stole my underwear once.

Welcome to Rosewood

I should have felt insulated and safe in the back of the Town Car.

Instead, my heart was pounding like crazy as the driver pulled into the long circular drive that would bring me to the front of the Rosewood Academy for Academic Excellence — my new home for the next ten months. The windows of the car were tinted, so no one could see in, but as I was in one of several limos (mixed in with Range Rovers, Audis, Mercedes' and other cars of the famous and wealthy), no one really paid attention. And, gauging by the chaos on the front lawn of the school campus — registration, moving in, laughing and getting reacquainted — people were too wrapped up in their own stuff to notice a new girl, anyway.

The new girl.

I sighed and gave myself a couple moments to calm my nerves as the driver rolled to a stop at the curb. I took my long brown hair out of the ponytail holder, then second-guessed and put it back in again. Then realized it would look sloppy to have a ponytail, so I took it out one last time.

God, Brooklyn, get it together.

The driver put the car into park, turned halfway toward me and smiled. "This is it."

"Yeah," I said, glancing out at the crowd. There were several tables, including one with a banner that read, "Check in. Come here first." Brilliant. At least *that* part was sorted. The fitting in and making friends part couldn't possibly be quite so easy.

"It will be fine," the driver assured me, as though he was reading my mind and standing in as my father or something, making me feel guilty that I'd forgotten his name already. "I hear it's a good school."

I almost snorted at his comment; Rosewood wasn't a *good*

school. Rosewood was the *best* school. The school governors and celebrities send their kids to. The place where no one asks how much the tuition is, because if you send your kid here, you can afford whatever it is and don't care what it costs, as long as your child is getting the best education money can buy. Of course, this isn't what the brochure says, it's what I heard my dad tell my grandmother when he phoned to tell her he was sending me back to the States. He said he didn't feel I was getting a quality education at my last school in London. Which is kind of ridiculous, because I'm pretty sure the Brits *invented* proper education, right?

Looking up at the big building now, I had seriously mixed feelings; I'd never been a huge fan of the school in London or maybe being in London altogether, and getting away from my parents was a distinct benefit. They were still there; probably it would be another year before they would move back to the States (though they promised to come for Christmas). But I knew exactly no one here at this school, and my old friends from before I left the U.S. were states away in Colorado, not exactly close enough to meet up for pizza on the weekend. And anyway, after two years away, we probably weren't really friends anymore. We'd become what Mom called "Christmas Card Friends"—meaning we caught up like once a year and didn't care for the other three-sixty-four.

At least in London I had some friends. Not super close ones, but still, friends I'd had to leave behind and would probably never see again who would *also* become "Christmas Card Friends". At least I didn't have a boyfriend I had to worry about leaving. No, leaving a boy behind had never been an issue for me; on the contrary, I was pretty much boy-repellent. Not that I was ugly or anything, I just wasn't the fun girl or the popular girl. I was the *plain* girl: brown hair and eyes, a few freckles across my nose, average build. Not overly smart, not overly pretty: the girl no one noticed.

But as I looked out at the crowd consisting of what would be my fellow students, I thought maybe I could change that. Maybe this would be the opportunity to reinvent myself that I'd been too chicken to take when we moved to London. Back then, I'd been shy and insecure; starting at a new school in a different country will do that. But now, I was back on home soil and could, as Dad would say, 'fake it till I made it'. And since Dad had paid whatever ridiculous amount of tuition it had cost to send me here, I had just as much right to be here as anyone else. I had no reason to be insecure or feel like I didn't belong here.

We came from old money that had little to do with my dad, even though he was a high ranking military strategist and probably made a lot of money at it. I think my coming back to the States for school had more to do with *that* than my education. A lot of Dad's job is classified, and based on all the recent late night and closed-door whispering on the phone and with Mom, I got the impression he was going out on a *very* classified assignment. My brother Robert, older by almost three years, was already far away at Yale doing his MBA, so I was their most immediate concern.

It would be easy for me to take it personally that they were sending me away, but I knew a lot of what they did was for my own safety. It had always been that way for Robert and me.

We weren't even allowed to use our real last name; Dad said if terrorists or other bad people knew who we were, they could use us to get to him and that made us a liability. I was so used to having a fake last name, I barely remembered my real one anymore.

It sounds cool and all spy-thriller, but trust me, after seventeen years of growing up with a military strategist, I knew it was mostly meetings, sitting around, and waiting for stuff to happen that almost never does. I can't talk about what assignments my dad has been on, but some of them were really big deals that were sort of world security things. But even those required a lot of sitting around and meetings.

Still, despite my dad's cool-sounding job, I was certainly no celebutante, although thinking about how I might actually end up rooming with one made my right eye twitch. But there was nothing for it and I couldn't stay in the Town Car forever.

Even as I thought this, the trunk popped open behind me.

I took a breath.

"Let me help you with your things," the driver said, getting out of the front seat and hurrying to open my door. As I stepped out onto the driveway with my backpack and my carry-on suitcase, he moved to the back of the car, grunting as he hauled out my steamer trunk. I looked around for a cart or something, suddenly worried that this poor man was going to have to haul my year's worth of clothes up what looked like at least fifteen stairs just to get to the main floor door. I had no idea where my room might be, but I hoped The Rosewood Academy for Academic Excellence had an elevator if it was anything beyond the ground floor.

It was the least the school could do, since it was lacking the one thing I argued with my parents was the most essential requirement to a girl's social development: boys.

Seychelles

That's right: The Rosewood Academy for Academic Excellence is an all-girls school. Because "part of receiving the best education money can buy is the lack of distractions," Dad had said. On some level I got his point and of course, I wanted to get good marks, but how was I supposed to grow into a functioning young woman without ever being able to interact with boys?

But as I looked around, there were a lot of boys. And I'm not talking old, bearded professors with tweed elbow patches, I'm talking young guys. Cute guys, milling around, moving luggage up into the building, chatting with girls. Maybe Dad was wrong.

"Can I help you with that, Sir?"

I swiveled around out of my reverie as one of the guys spoke to the limo driver. This boy was definitely cute and had nothing professorly about him at all. He looked a bit young, maybe fifteen or so; too young for me, but in a couple of years, with those big brown eyes and that friendly, open smile, he was going to be a heartbreaker.

The limo driver looked suddenly relieved. "Thanks. Maybe you could help me take this up to…" he looked pointedly at me as though I had any idea where my assigned room was.

"Oh! I guess I have to check in." I glanced over to the Check In booth. "Let's start there."

Without another word, the boy nodded, grabbed a handle and picked up an end of the trunk, his biceps bulging a bit at the effort. For a kid, he was pretty cut. I hoped his upper classmates subscribed to the same Phys Ed program. Realizing I was supposed to be the lead on this caravan of three, I stopped ogling, picked up my carry-on, jogged a few steps to get around them and led them over to the Check In booth. There were several other girls standing in front of me, so I motioned for the boy and the driver to put my trunk down.

The driver glanced at his car but didn't say anything. Experience told me that people who wear livery uniforms had politeness built right in, as though it came on a hanger with the black suit and cap.

"You can go," I said. "I know you have other clients."

He looked at me, indecision on his face.

"Really," I assured him, waving at the boy beside me. "I'm sure I'll find plenty of help. Thanks for getting me here safely."

"Thank you," he said. "Sunday afternoons are my busy time, taking the weekend commuters to the airport." He extended his hand and shook mine. Then, with a polite nod of his head, he turned and left.

So this is awkward, I thought as I stood there for the next several moments, the kid who'd helped with my trunk standing next to me, not saying anything either. I figured I should at least thank him, but when I opened my mouth, I was interrupted by a very authoritative-looking girl with a clipboard who'd materialized by my side. She had long reddish-brown hair, knotted up in a messy ponytail that left wisps framing her round face. She had what my mom would have called 'baby fat', but wore nice jeans and a white blouse under a standard-issue navy blazer which looked identical to the three packed in my trunk. She also had a pretty scarf tied around her neck in a complicated knot, reminding me of one of my mother's bridge friends who never left the house without a Hermes scarf accenting one of her many Chanel suits. It was weird to see a scarf on a teenager, but this girl sort of rocked it and I was strangely envious.

"I need you," she said and I was about to beg her pardon, when I realized she was talking to the guy. She pointed to the girl at the front of the line. "She's got luggage in her car. Go help her, okay?"

The guy gave me an apologetic look and then took off before I even had a chance to thank him for his help.

Clipboard girl smiled at me and then jutted her chin toward my trunk. "Don't worry, I'll get you some muscle when you're ready to move in."

"Thanks," I said. "I'm Brooklyn Prescott."

She smiled again, "I know. I'm the orientation coordinator; they give me the files of all the new girls. Nice to meet you, Brooklyn. I'm Seychelles Spencer. But you can call me Chelly, sounds like Shelley, but spelled with a C-H. I'm a junior, too, so we'll definitely be getting to know each other." She hugged the clipboard to her chest with her left arm and stuck her right one out to shake hands.

"Seychelles? What a nice name." Thanks to Dad's job and both of my parents' love for travel, I had a pretty good knowledge of world geography. So although I'd never been there, I knew that Seychelles was a country made up of tropical islands near Madagascar in the middle of the Indian Ocean, known for its remote beauty.

She rolled her eyes. "I was conceived on my parents' honeymoon there. How's *that* for a name legacy?" She fake gagged, making me laugh. She also made me wonder (and not for the first time) if I got *my* name thanks to my parents conceiving me while traveling to New York City. Mom always said she loved New York, and I wasn't about to ask her, but you never know. Seychelles was so much more exotic, but maybe it was better I didn't know for sure that my name was thanks to some horny vacation sex while mom was extra fertile.

Ugh, I wasn't far behind with the fake gagging. Enough about that, though. I had more important things going on, and anyway, Seychelles was talking to me.

"I didn't realize you were British," she said. "I thought you were American?"

I smiled. "I am American, but I've been in London for a couple of years, so the accent sneaks in. It will wear off soon enough. My British friends still think I speak totally American, so I guess I sound funny to everyone."

"Well I for one think it's darling, *darling*," Chelly said in a drawl that I'm guessing she thought sounded British (but didn't). She also gave me a big wink. I liked her already and hoped we'd share some classes. Speaking of classmates…

13

"So, uh..." I said, looking around at the throng of students around us.

"Yes?"

"This is going to sound like a weird question..."

She waved me off. "I'm orientation coordinator; it's my job to answer all of your questions about Rosewood. Nothing is too weird."

I leaned in. "I thought there weren't supposed to be any boys here?"

Chelly stared at me for a second and then took a breath and looked around. "Right. Yeah, there are boys here today helping with move in. They're from the all-boys school a few miles from here: Westwood."

Oh. Well *that* was disappointing.

She nodded sympathetically and I realized I must have showed my disappointment on my face. "I know, it's a drag, right? But don't worry, there are lots of opportunities to hang out with them. Not the same as a co-ed school, of course, but you won't have to live like a nun for ten months." She winked and then her eyes widened. "Unless you want to, I mean, some girls...not to say you're a ..."

I laughed again and interrupted her stuttering when it sounded like she was just going to make it worse. "It's okay, I knew what you meant. It's not like I'm easy or anything, but it is nice to have guys around." I was hardly easy—I'd barely even gotten to second base.

Chelly waggled her eyebrows at me. "True story. Anyway, once you get checked in, we'll get your stuff up to your room. Newbie orientation and tour is tonight at seven after dinner, so don't bother trying to find your way around this afternoon—just get settled in for now." She glanced down at her clipboard. "Your roommate is Celia Thomas up on the third floor."

My heart fluttered. "Any relation to Kevin Thomas?"

A smile spread across Chelly's face. "The three-time Oscar Award winner?"

I held my breath but nodded.

"His niece."

Wow. Okay, I shouldn't have been quite so starstruck and Dad had warned me a lot of the kids here had famous and very important parents and that I shouldn't get all fangirl on them, but it was hard not to get excited about being the roommate of the niece of such a famous (and hot, let's be honest) actor.

"Seychelles!" someone hollered from one of the booths on the other side of the lawn. "We need you over here!"

Chelly gave me a shrug. "That's my cue; I'll see you tonight at orientation, if not before, okay? Welcome to Rosewood!"

And with that, she was gone. I turned back toward the front of the line in which I was now second, and thought about my first moments at Rosewood. Okay, so there were no guys, but if the other students were as nice as Chelly, I would do okay. And I was about to be the roommate of the niece of a VIP.

Or not.

Will

I finally got to the front of the line. I got checked in and was handed my room key and a map of the huge building in front of me with a highlighted trail from the front door to my room. Easy. Maybe too easy?

I was thanking the girl at the desk for her help and was about to look around for Chelly to assign me 'some muscle' to help with my trunk, when I was hit from behind, shoving me into the table and completely knocking the wind out of me.

"Oof," is the involuntary sound I made as all the air was pushed out of my lungs.

"Shoot, sorry!" came from behind me as I gasped for air and then turned, ready to give whoever had come plowing into me a few choice words.

But when I saw who had run into me, words and the sudden anger dissolved in my throat. Because the guy standing in front of me, breathing hard from, I guessed, running a marathon that didn't stop until my body got in the way, was gorgeous.

Like, movie star gorgeous. Zac Efron gorgeous.

And the sheepish smile and pleading raised eyebrows just made him that much more so. And then I wondered if he *was* a movie star, on campus at Westwood in between shoots or something. He didn't look familiar, but he sure had that look about him. He had messy brown hair that was a lot longer than the military cuts I was used to seeing on most of the guys in my life. Maybe it wasn't always messy, but it looked like it was suffering the effects of the aforesaid marathon. Honestly, in that second my fingers tingled, wanting to run through it or fix it or just *feel* it. *Something;* I was dying to touch it.

His mouth, turned up on the right in that killer smile which was obviously begging my forgiveness, was full and lush and made for kissing. And as I took in the shape of his lips, I realized in horror that I'd just licked my own.

I quickly lifted my eyes to his, which darted up to mine a half a second later. Busted, *he'd* been looking at *my* mouth, too.

Awkward. My face got hotter and redder and I kind of wanted to crawl under the check in table. But then I realized, unless I was having a stroke, impairing my vision, *he* was blushing, too. Which was pretty adorable in one of those high school teen movie moments.

But still, I stood there paralyzed, trying to get my brain with the program, because deep down somewhere, I knew social protocol dictated I say *something*.

Luckily, he came to the same conclusion. "I'm really sorry," he repeated. "I'm totally late; I was supposed to be here like an hour ago, but I was helping this freshman get himself moved in and as I was running up, I tripped and..." he gestured toward me and took a deep breath, still huffing a little from his run.

"You ran into me," I said. Like it wasn't obvious what had happened. But I said it with a smile, like he hadn't knocked the wind out of me. Although even if he hadn't, I had a feeling just meeting him would have rendered me breathless. As it was, my heart was racing and not just from the physical contact.

"Right. Like I said, sorry about that."

I waved him off. "So you're here to help with luggage?" I asked, holding my breath as I waited for his answer.

Suddenly, he did a big flourish with his right hand, bowed in front of me and said, in a very stiff and British voice, "Willmont Leander Gareth Davidson at your service, ma'am."

I couldn't help the smile. "That's your name?" It sounded like a stuffy old man's name. Not that I would have said that out loud, but all he was missing was "The thiiiiiiird" drawled at the end.

He saluted and clicked his heels together. "Indeed, ma'am."

I laughed, suddenly picturing him in a livery outfit. Cute *and* funny? This guy was a heartbreaker for sure. I bet he even had a six-pack to round out the package. "Willmont," I said, trying it out.

He cringed and gave his head a shake.

"Will?" I tried, giving him a sideways glance.

He looked up, as if considering it. "Better, I guess," he announced and then ripped the map out of my hand. He glanced at it and then at the front of the school. "Third floor?" he groaned. "I bet the girl behind you is on the ground floor; I should have been a few minutes later."

I felt instantly guilty and it was my turn to apologize. "Sorry. Isn't there an elevator?"

He frowned at me and then made a big show of flexing his arms like a bodybuilder, not that I could see any muscles through his Westwood Academy sweatshirt, but my imagination could fill in the blanks. "How am I supposed to impress all the new girls if I use the elevator? Hmmm?"

"You'll just have to do it with your wit and charm." *And by the way, mission accomplished*, I didn't say.

He rolled his eyes and then gave me an incredulous look. "Nice try. I know your type. You're all into caveman displays of strength and virility."

"Hardly," I said, silently cursing that my voice broke on the single word.

"Whatever," he said and bent to grab a handle of my trunk, the weight of which obviously surprised him. "Jesus, are you sneaking your boyfriend in here, or something?"

"No! I don't have a boyfriend," I blurted out. Ugh. *Smooth one, Brooklyn. Like this guy is* really *interested.* There was no way on this planet earth that this guy wasn't already taken, with like fifteen girls in the wings.

He glanced at me, obviously amused, and then looked away, scanning the crowd. Probably for his girlfriend…

"Hey Jenks!" He hollered, looking toward another guy in a Westwood hoodie who was talking to Chelly as she consulted her clipboard. "Jenks!" he repeated. "Over here."

Jenks (First name? Last name? Nickname?) finally looked up at Will, nodding before turning back to Chelly. He said something to her and then nudged her gently with his elbow

18

before coming over. The way Chelly smiled and watched him walk away from her, it was obvious she was checking out his butt and liking what she saw. I could hardly blame her (were *all* the guys from Westwood movie-star beautiful?) but it was a bit embarrassing, nonetheless. I caught her eye and she winked, obviously not quite as embarrassed. Maybe Jenks was her boyfriend; that little elbow nudge he gave her was telling and I couldn't exclude the possibility that they were a couple.

She sure could do worse; tall and ginger, with his Prince Harry good looks and a butt I hadn't yet seen, but was Chelly-approved, he certainly held his own in the cute guy category.

"Grab the other side, would you?" Will said as he leaned down again to grab the steamer trunk handle.

"Where to?" Jenks asked, looking at me, not yet making a move to help Will with the trunk.

"Third floor," Will answered for me before I could open my mouth. "South wing."

Jenks groaned but then suddenly turned toward me. "We haven't met, so I'm going to assume you *didn't* choose a room at the very end of the third floor just to torture us."

The old, shy Brooklyn would have fallen over herself to apologize over the location of her room (which I had no control over) but the new Brooklyn decided she wanted to flirt a little more with this very cute boy in front of her. And his friend.

I glanced at Will before looking Jenks in the eye and saying, "As a matter of fact, I did it just so you boys could impress me with displays of your strength and virility. I am a cavewoman at heart, after all. Carry on." I waved at the trunk, feigning impatience.

Jenks looked at me like I was insane, but Will barked out a laugh, making me feel clever and a little bit powerful. "I like you," he said, picking up the trunk. "Come on, Jenks, you heard the lady...er...cavewoman."

Before picking up the trunk, Jenks turned to me and stuck out his hand. "Evan Jenkins, since that clod over there didn't see fit to introduce us."

"Hey," Will said. "I would have."

We both turned and looked at him, waiting.

"Evan Jenkins, this is…" he looked at me for help, since he must have realized in that second I hadn't told him my name.

I smirked and held out my hand. "Brooklyn Prescott. Nice to meet you."

Evan smiled. "Likewise. Now let's get this ridiculously heavy trunk upstairs."

"Brooklyn," Will said, like he was considering my name, the same way I had his only moments before. "I like it."

"I'm glad it meets your approval," I said, enjoying our banter.

"Come on, you two," Evan protested, picking up his end of the trunk. "You can flirt on the way."

I almost choked on my own saliva.

Running ahead of them so I wouldn't have to respond to Evan's remark or worse, acknowledge it in front of Will, I led the boys up the concrete stairs, through the open doorway and into the Rosewood main building.

From the research I'd done online when my parents told me I'd be attending, I knew the dorms were in this main building, along with administrative offices, dining hall and some of the smaller classrooms. Behind it was the rest of the campus, scattered about in several stone buildings, many that were smaller copies of this one. There was also a running track, baseball diamonds, soccer fields and a whole indoor sports complex, with an Olympic sized pool, squash courts and a full gym. Not to mention the stables—what I was most excited about. I'd had to give up my equestrian lessons when we'd left the States—Mom refused to drive in England, and with Dad always off at his meetings, I was stuck without any way to get to stables. But now that I was attending a school with horses, I was eager to get back into riding.

"The service elevator is just up there on the right," Evan said from behind me as I stepped into the marbled lobby, his voice echoing off the high ceilings.

I turned to look at the boys and shook my head. "You're going to use the lift? Really? So much for impressing me."

"Screw that," Evan said, smirking. "I'll impress you with my appreciation for modern technologies." He jerked the thumb of his free hand toward Will. "If Mr. Dark Ages wants to impress you, he can haul your trunk up the two flights of stairs on his own. And," he gave Will a wide-eyed look. "May I remind you those two flights each have landings—fourteen foot ceilings, and all."

Amused, I glanced at Will.

"Dude," he said shaking his head. "I don't want to make you look bad when I put this thing over my head and carry it up the stairs like Atlas. I wouldn't do that to you; we can use the elevator."

Then he looked at me and winked.

Rendering me speechless.

Celia

As it was move-in day for everyone on campus, we had to wait our turn for the elevator, which meant more time with Evan and Will, which I was definitely okay with. The way the guys joked with each other, it was obvious they were friends, which made it even more fun to hang around with them. And it sort of took the pressure off me to carry a conversation. A good thing, since being with them was a bit overwhelming.

They did ask about me some, though, surprised to find out I'm American.

"But that accent," Will said. "It's so…"

"Dodgy?" I finished for him.

"Charming," Evan said at the same time.

Will shook his head and stared into my eyes. "Sexy," he said. I had to look away, unable to handle the intensity in his gaze. If he was flirting with me like Evan had said, I loved it, but it was a little overwhelming at the same time. I'd never been drunk, but maybe this is what it felt like; like my insides were vibrating and I wanted to jump up and down. In private, of course.

Still, I was beginning to really understand what made girls get stupid over attention from guys. Will was definitely making me feel like I could get stupid over him.

Luckily, the elevator arrived at that moment, the ding interrupting the tension between us. The guys picked up the trunk and shuffled into the elevator car, putting it down, so they could turn around. I entered last with my backpack and carry-on spinner, turning around quickly to face the door so I wouldn't have to look at Will, but as the halves met together, I realized it was mirrored. Will caught my eye and smiled. I looked down at my hand resting on the handle of my luggage, silently willing my heart to stop thudding in my chest, because I was almost sure he and Evan could hear it.

Next thing I knew, there was a soft rustle of clothing and Will was pressing his hand on my shoulder, his scent—part cologne, part laundry, part *boy*—wafting over me until I had no choice but to breathe in deeper, my nostrils flaring. My head turned toward him and I almost fell into a daze, sure he was going to pull me into his arms. Waiting, hoping.

That's when I realized what he was *actually* doing; I'd forgotten to push the button for the third floor and he'd leaned over me to do it.

How utterly humiliating.

"Sorry," he said as the elevator jerked into motion. "I didn't think you'd want to be stuck in here all day."

"Of course not," I said, my voice cracking as I shook my head and spit out an excuse. "I was worrying about my schedule. Sorry to be daft."

Finally, after what felt like the longest ride in the history of lifts, we were let out on the third floor. Evan told me to turn left and I preceded them to the very last room on the right. I knocked, but then remembered my key card and slid it into the reader, the light turning green and unlocking the door with a soft 'shunk'.

With a held breath I pushed open the door, super excited and nervous to meet my new roommate, the famous-adjacent, Celia Thomas. But the room was empty. Of people, at least. It seemed to be a lot more filled and decorated than it should have been for one person. *Apparently almost-famous girls have a lot of stuff and like to spread out*, I thought.

"So, where do you want this?" Evan asked, grunting as they pivoted to get through the doorway with the trunk.

I moved deeper into the room, put my bags on the unmade mattress and stood to the side so they could get past me. There wasn't a lot of room for the three of us to maneuver, but I pointed to the one spot on the floor that was big enough to accommodate the trunk and watched as they lowered it into place.

"Very impressive," I said. "Even though you used the lift."

Evan gave me an amused look while Will rolled his shoulders.

"Thank you both. Really. I do appreciate your help."

"Anytime," Will said, winking at me again and then opening his mouth as though to say something, but was suddenly interrupted by a girl coming into the room, pushing past him to stand in front of me.

She was stunning, with her *cafe-au-lait* complexion and the kind of curly brown with multi-colored highlights hair that people paid a lot of money for in salons. I had a millisecond to wonder if her striking blue eyes were that color thanks to contacts, before I realized they were trained on me. And not in a good way.

"Uh, hello?" the girl said, her face mashed up into a frown that made me want to hide in the tiny closet. Everyone hears about mean-girl celebutante-zillas, but you hope your roommate at a super-exclusive boarding school isn't going to be one.

So much for that. Without a word, Evan disappeared and Will gave me a wave before he ducked out too, leaving me alone with the girl who I supposed was Celia. Cowards. Not that I could blame them...

Taking a deep breath, I forced myself to smile and stuck out my hand. "Hi, I'm Brooklyn, your new roommate. You can call me Brook, though." Almost no one called me Brook, but in that second, I was desperate for her to like me and the nickname fell out of my mouth.

"*You're* not my roommate," the girl said, glancing at my outstretched hand and ignoring it. "Kaylee is my roommate."

I just blinked at her. Tears pooled in the corners of my eyes, though I begged them not to fall—nothing could be worse than bawling in front of my (maybe) new roommate on my first day here.

She exhaled and rolled her eyes. "Stupid registrar's office. Kaylee enrolled late because her parents were on location in Africa, but Kaylee and I are *always* roommates. It's nothing

24

personal."

"Oh," I said, still willing myself not to cry. Celia didn't seem mad at me, but it kind of hurt to be rejected anyway.

"It's okay. It's just a mix-up," Celia said, slipping an arm across my shoulder and giving me a reassuring squeeze. "We'll get it worked out. Didn't you notice all her things were already here?"

I looked around the room with new eyes. *Duh, Brooklyn.* "I guess. I sort of thought maybe you just had a lot of stuff."

She laughed. "I do have a lot of stuff, but not this much." She swiveled me toward the door. "Leave your stuff here and let's go back down and get this sorted out. I'm sorry that you got all the way up here with all your things, but we'll figure this out."

I looked at her beside me and smiled; she was being very *un*celebutante-zilla-like. "Thanks. Really."

She shrugged. "Don't mention it. You're one of us now. Rosewoods look after each other."

Settling In

Forty-five minutes later, my key card had been reprogrammed and a couple of different guys had followed me up to Celia's room to move my trunk the four rooms away to my new (confirmed!) home for my stay at Rosewood. My new roommate, Emmeline Somerville, hadn't arrived yet, so after much agonizing over the decision, I made the choice of taking the slightly less desirable bed on the left (the shared closet was on my side, so she'd have a bit more room for her stuff).

Now that I was settling into my room, I was on my own until dinner. Celia had said I could come back and hang out with her and Kaylee, but although the new Brooklyn really wanted to, the old Brooklyn thought it was a good idea to unpack and not force herself on the other girls.

And anyway, the dorm rooms weren't big enough to store trunks in, so I needed to get everything out of mine. The orientation package said any large luggage could be tagged and put out in the hall to be taken to storage. I didn't want it to be in Emmeline's way when she did finally show up, so getting the trunk unpacked was a priority.

I didn't know anything about Emmeline, other than her name and that she was flying in from Paris, or maybe Venice (there had been some debate about that at the check in booth) and may not arrive until very late. I'd been dying to ask Chelly and Celia about her, but it seemed kind of catty.

Since she was entering her third year at Rosewood, Emmeline wasn't required at orientation, but I got the feeling all the other girls were expected to have still arrived by dinnertime, although Emmeline, or perhaps her family, were held to a different standard.

Which was pretty intimidating. I was nervous enough, but with each passing moment as I unpacked and organized all my things, my anxiety over my new roommate ratcheted up. Sure, all the girls had been really nice so far, but meeting your new roommate is a big deal and I didn't want to screw it up.

At 5:45 she still hadn't arrived, but dinner was at six, so I quickly finished up and tugged my trunk out into the hall. With map in hand, I headed to the main stairs to go down to the dining room, which was on the main floor. But I wasn't alone — the hallway was filled with girls, and I was suddenly swarmed, since I was the new girl. It seemed the third floor was all juniors, so everyone knew each other from prior years and all wanted to meet me. I introduced myself and tried to remember the names and faces of all the girls around me. There were one-hundred girls in each grade at Rosewood, so it was going to take some time before I'd know them all.

It got a bit overwhelming, but suddenly I heard my name from behind me.

I turned and there was Celia, walking toward me and the throng of other students. "Girls! Leave Brooklyn alone — she just got here. You'll all get to meet her; you have all year!"

She gave me a broad smile and hooked her arm through mine. "Kaylee's finishing getting dressed, but I wanted to make sure you were settled in and found your way to the dining room."

I held up the paper I'd gotten from the check in desk. "I have my map."

Celia started walking down the hall, gently tugging me along next to her as other girls fell in line around us. "You don't need a map; you have us. So, tell us more about you."

Orientation

As we ate dessert, a very young-looking teacher at the front of the room (the entire faculty sat together at two long tables) got up and walked over to a raised podium. He looked very focused on the floor in front of him and I wondered if he was nervous. A buzz of whispers and hushed conversations erupted through the dining hall.

I turned to Celia. "What's going on?"

She looked up to the front of the room. "Evening announcements. Newbie teacher." She squinted. "Newbie *cute* teacher." She nudged Kaylee on her other side, who also looked up from her fruit salad.

"Nice," she said. "I wonder what he's teaching."

"I bet he could teach me a few things," Chelly said from across the table.

We all laughed and watched as the new teacher adjusted the microphone and started talking. No sound came out and someone hollered at him to turn it on. He stared blankly out at the crowd and then clued in, switching the mic on. He cleared his throat and started again. It was kind of adorable.

"Good evening. My name is Jeffrey Stratton...er...Mr. Stratton. As the newest addition to the faculty, I have been given the honor of welcoming you all here to The Rosewood Academy for Academic Excellence. Most of you are returning students and I welcome you all back, but I'd also like to extend a special welcome to our first year students. Welcome!"

"How many times can one person say, 'welcome'?" Kaylee mumbled.

"We could make it a drinking game," Celia said.

Kaylee snickered and I looked around, wondering if these girls really did drink. Sure, I'd had some pints back in London, but I was hoping to get into a good journalism program at

Syracuse or Northwestern, and that meant good grades. I was taking the Academic Excellence part of The Rosewood Academy for Academic Excellence very seriously. Which meant although I wanted to have a good time, I was going to have to limit the partying.

"I wonder if he's married," Chelly mused, looking up at the podium with dreamy eyes.

"He's a *teacher*," Celia reminded her.

Chelly gave Celia a look. "He looks like a *student* teacher, so what, like, twenty max. That's only three years. Nothing. My father is twelve years older than my mother." She turned back to look at the teacher in question again. "And anyway, just look at him."

We all did. And I had to admit, even if just to myself, that he *was* hot. Even from our table, I could tell by the angles of his masculine face, and his dark-rimmed glasses that gave him something of a geeky chic look. He had broad shoulders under his blazer and slim hips in his chinos. And his voice, low and soothing despite his nervousness (which just made him cuter), made me hope I would be in one of his classes; I could listen to that voice all day.

"...in the library at eight. Students new to Rosewood are asked to meet here at the podium at the conclusion of these announcements for orientation and grounds tour."

Oops! I realized I'd zoned out and hadn't really been listening to what he'd said, but at least I'd caught that last part. Chelly nodded at me. "That's us."

Cute teacher wrapped up his speech: "So that's it for me, everyone. I hope to see you out in the science labs when classes start tomorrow. Until then, thanks for your attention and again, welcome!"

We all laughed, but applauded as was expected. The buzz around the room told us we weren't the only group of girls who were hoping to have him as a science teacher.

I pushed the rest of my dessert away and looked at Chelly. "Shall we?"

29

She nodded as she shoved a cookie in her mouth. "Mmm. Just give me a sec, I'm sublimating my need to kiss that hot teacher with food."

"Didn't you get any over the summer?" Kaylee asked.

Chelly shrugged. "A bit here and there. But you know how it is. I can't wait for the first dance next week."

"Aren't you with Evan Jenkins?" I asked, remembering how I'd seen them together earlier.

She looked at me blankly. "Jenks?"

"You seemed to be close this afternoon."

"He's cute," Celia said.

"He's totally cute," Chelly said but frowned at me. "Did he seem like he was into me?"

She seemed really unsure, which was a bit odd, since he'd *totally* looked like he was into her. "Yeah," I said. "He did. The way he was smiling at you and nudged you before he came to help me with my stuff."

Chelly gave a half-smile. "Huh. I guess I didn't notice."

"It was pretty busy with everyone moving in; you had other things on your mind," Celia said.

"True enough," Chelly said. "But now I'm looking forward to the dance even more."

"So you're going to go for him?" I asked. "He seems nice; I think he'd make a good boyfriend."

The other girls laughed. I looked around at them, hoping someone would let me in on the joke. "What?" I asked when no one did.

Chelly leaned in close. "The last thing I'm looking for is a steady boyfriend." The way she said steady boyfriend was the same way a chef would say, "spoiled meat."

"That dance is going to be like a Westwood buffet," Chelly continued. "And Seychelles is hungry."

I laughed with the rest of the girls, but secretly hoped Will wasn't going to end up as a dish on her menu.

~❤~

Since Chelly was the orientation coordinator, she had to stay with the groups of freshmen while I got paired up with a sophomore named Andrea, who took me around campus and showed me where all my classes would be. After the busy day and the loud dining hall, it was nice to have a quiet one-on-one tour of the campus.

"So I guess that's it," she said when we had circled around to the front lobby of the main building.

"What about the stables?" I asked.

She shrugged. "They're not on the tour. They're out back beside the sports complex; it's kind of obvious where they are."

"Can we go see them?"

She slipped her cell out of her pocket and pressed a button before frowning at me. "Uh, I'm meeting a friend in ten minutes, but if you are okay you can go on your own, if you want. After this, it's free time."

"Okay," I said. "Thanks so much for the tour."

Andrea smiled. "You're welcome. Well, see you around!" And then she was gone.

I looked down at my map and found the best door to take to get out to the stables. I ducked out, suddenly glad I'd worn a sweatshirt since it had gotten brisk out as the sun had started to set. Rushing over to the stables, I hoped they weren't locked and I could get inside; although everyone had been really nice so far, I craved the quiet of the stables and couldn't wait to meet some of the horses.

The small door on the side was unlocked and I pushed it open, calling out a "Hello?" as I did. A friendly nicker greeted me from one of the stalls, but no human voices. I stepped inside, taking a deep breath, allowing the familiar smells to fill my lungs; I'd always had a love for horses and riding, so just the warm, earthy aromas of the stables were enough to take me to a happy place.

Turning the corner into the main hall, my heart swelled as I looked down the aisle and was met by the turned heads of several horses. The friendly one nickered again and I stepped quietly to the first stall where a beautiful bay was stretching his neck out toward me. I reached my hand out to pet him.

"Not that one," said someone behind me, scaring me half to death.

I gasped and spun around to see a guy leaning casually against a large push broom as he smiled my way.

"You startled me," I said.

He shrugged one shoulder. "Sorry, I didn't mean to, but you were probably about to get bit. I figured you'd want to avoid that."

I glanced back at the horse I'd been about to touch. He looked innocent enough, gazing at me with his chocolaty brown eyes and long lashes.

"I know, he looks like a peach," the guy said, pushing his broom across the floor, kicking up dust. "But that's how he draws you in and then CHOMP, he's taken a chunk out of you. He's mean."

"So why's he here?" I asked.

The dark-haired guy, who wore faded jeans and a gray long-sleeved t-shirt with the Rosewood logo on it, pushed his broom again, the bristles making a swishing noise across the floor. "Just is." Then he looked up at me. "Why are *you* here?"

The way he looked at me, almost through me, made me look away. "I don't know. It's been a long time since I've been around horses and I guess I missed them."

Swish, swish, swish.

"So you work here?" I asked, realizing it was a lame question with an obvious answer, but I felt like I needed to fill the silence and that was all my brain could come up with on short notice.

"Seems so," he said. *Swish, swish, swish.* "Name's Brady."

I stepped over to him and stuck out my hand. "I'm Brooklyn. Nice to meet you."

As his large, warm hand enveloped mine, I looked into his eyes and realized he wasn't that old; maybe eighteen or nineteen.

"Brooklyn, like the borough?"

I tried not to think too hard about it, remembering how Chelly said she got her name. "Yes."

"That's nice."

"Thank you," I said, pulling my eyes away from his intense gaze, realizing as I did that he was still holding my hand. I took it out of his grasp and turned back toward the horses. "So which ones can I touch?"

I heard a gentle clatter and realized he'd put the broom down. "Come," he said as he walked past me toward the horses. I didn't think but to follow him.

He stopped at the first stall, giving the bay a wide berth. "This is Sir Lancelot, a.k.a. Sir Bitesalot, steer clear."

I smiled and nodded. "Got it."

He pointed across the way but I had to peek in through the door to see the horse standing at the back of the stall who looked like she was dozing. "That's Proud Mary; she's sweet, but old. Mostly she's retired."

He moved to the next set of doors. "This fine roan is Charlie. He's a real ladies man." Brady confidently placed his palm on the nose of the curious horse who nodded his head, like he knew he was being talked about and heartily agreed.

I laughed. "You've got him pegged."

I stepped closer and lay my own palm on the velvet muzzle. Charlie nickered and nuzzled my hand. I looked up at Brady who, I realized, was standing very close. "I see what you mean."

He smiled down at me. "Told you. Next thing you know, the two of you will be riding off into the sunset. He knows how to treat a lady, that's for sure."

"We're not that complicated," I said. "Ladies, that is. Guys just need to figure out what we want and then when they deliver, we're putty." *Where did that come from?* I wondered, but held his gaze.

Brady's eyes widened for half a second and his tanned face suddenly looked a bit more ruddy than it had a second ago, but he didn't say anything. I liked that I was able to make him blush. And I was starting to think I was getting good at this flirting thing; first Will and now this guy.

He stepped to the next stall and stopped, waiting for me to follow. I gave Charlie a final pat and caught up. "This is Poppy and across the way is her best friend, Daisy. They're both sweethearts and great for beginners, which I'm guessing you're not."

I shook my head. "Eight years of lessons."

"English or Western?"

"English. Dressage. Five blue ribbons." Yes, I was bragging, and maybe the blue ribbons were won at my own stable's tiny events, but they still counted — it's not like this guy was going to track them down.

His eyebrows lifted as he nodded. "Impressive. Are you going to be on the team here?"

My heart fluttered a little at the thought of joining a team and competing. I was a bit rusty, but had been pretty good back in the day. "I just arrived today, but I didn't know there was one. Who is the coach?"

"Fleming. You'll like him, but he's tough. Sign up at the office. During business hours, of course," he added. "He'll want to talk to you about your background and experience."

"Thanks, well, I guess I should get back. And I don't want to keep you," I said; he probably wanted to finish up and get home as it was getting late. I gave Poppy's soft nose a rub, laughing as she smacked her lips together playfully.

"Good to meet you, Brooklyn."

I looked up. "And you," I said, giving him a smile, noticing his eyes were the oddest shade of amber that were set off by his black hair. He was quite striking. Beautiful, even.

I realized I was staring and turned away quickly. "Thanks again. See you around," I said and quickly left, hearing the *swish, swish* resume as I gently closed the door behind me.

Emmeline

It had been probably the most exhausting day of my life, save the day I moved to London and had jet lag on top of the whole ordeal of moving overseas. But starting a new school, being introduced to a bunch of new girls, unpacking, touring aforementioned new school, not to mention meeting the guy of your dreams, will wear you out completely.

So when your dorm room door swings open at two a.m., showering you with light from the hallway, you wake up from a dead sleep and have no idea where you are and who might be coming to attack you.

Luckily for the people in the rooms next to yours, you might even be so out of it that you forget to scream.

But after a couple of bleary-eyed blinks and a good yawn to get some oxygen to my brain, I realized the girl who had busted into my room had to be none other than my new roommate, Emmeline Somerville. And judging by the shapes behind her, her parents.

I sat up in bed, pulling the comforter up to my neck, not sure what to even say.

"Uh hi," was my opener.

The light went on, causing me to squint for a moment.

"Sorry," Emmeline (?) said in a very curt tone. "We had hoped not to be this late."

"It was unavoidable," the woman behind her added.

I nodded, still clutching the covers. As my eyes adjusted to the light, I took in my roommate as she drifted into the room. She looked exactly like what you would expect a trust-fund debutante to look like, although a bit disheveled after what must have been at least an entire day of travel. Her complexion looked just about perfect and her eye makeup looked better after who knows how many hours than mine looked five minutes after applying it. Her blond hair was knotted up in what looked like a very complicated twist, soft wisps framing her face and allowing her diamond earrings to show. She wore a diamond necklace to match and a dress that looked casual, but probably cost hundreds, if not thousands of dollars off the rack. Even more than the rest of the girls at Rosewood, this girl oozed money.

And attitude.

Awesome.

I swallowed and ran my tongue around my teeth before I introduced myself. I should have shaken her parents' hands, but I wasn't about to get out of the bed wearing only a t-shirt and underwear. "I'm Brooklyn Prescott."

The woman stepped over to me and shook my hand, "Mrs. Somerville and this is Emmeline and my husband, Mr. Somerville," she indicated her husband who was arranging two enormous suitcases inside the door.

"Nice to meet you," I said, but she'd already turned to her daughter and her father didn't bother looking my way.

"We paid for a single room for you, Emmeline," he said as he finished with the luggage and stood up.

Single room? I didn't even know that was an option.

Emmeline huffed out a breath and looked like she was about to say something, but Mrs. Somerville interrupted. "Why are we major benefactors of this school, if we can't be assured our daughter has a private room?"

"Mother..."

"I'll call the dean," Mrs. Somerville said digging into her purse. I couldn't believe she was planning to call the dean *now*.

"*Mother.* I'm exhausted," Emmeline snapped.

"Fine, I'll do it in the morning."

Emmeline turned to her father. "Thank you for bringing my things up."

He nodded and leaned over to kiss her cheek. "We'll get this straightened out in the morning."

Emmeline nodded. "Fine. Thank you both for bringing me and for the summer in Europe. See you at Christmas."

Her mother shook her head. "No, honey, we'll be on the world cruise. But we can Skype."

"Right," Emmeline said, looking not the least bit disappointed. "I forgot. I'll speak to you soon."

Pulling her into a stiff hug, Mrs. Somerville looked at me over her shoulder when she said, "Yes. And we'll get you out of this room as soon as we can."

Which told me pretty much everything I needed to know about Emmeline Somerville. Without another word, I pulled the covers over my head and rolled toward the wall.

My alarm buzzed at 6:45 and as I reached for it to turn it off, I realized my groan was joined by another from across the room.

It almost scared the bejeepers out of me, until I remembered the night before. And Emmeline.

I peeked across the room and blinked as I realized she was staring back at me.

"Hi," she said, sounding even more tired than she looked, which was quite the accomplishment.

"Hi," I said back, cautious.

"Sorry. It was really late last night and now I forget your name."

I wasn't sure why it mattered since one of us was leaving, but I answered her anyway. "Brooklyn Prescott."

"I'm Emmeline."

Manners dictated I acknowledge her with a *'nice to meet you'*, but I was having some trouble getting the words out. I simply nodded and pushed the covers off me. "I guess I'll see about getting my trunk brought up."

She didn't get up, but moved her head, cocking it so she could look up at me now that I was standing. "Why?"

"Because one of us is leaving, and I'm guessing it will be me." *Unless you're moving to some sort of palace suite*, I didn't say. I turned away from her, heading to the bathroom, the one where

I'd been so careful not to take up too much space with my things. All for nothing.

"Wait!" she said, her tone sharp.

I crossed my arms over my chest.

She sat up, the comforter falling, exposing her tank top and pooling in her lap. I was shocked to realize she'd made her bed—I would have just flopped down on the bare mattress if I'd come in so late after a whole day of travel.

Maybe even more surprising was that I'd been able to sleep through it all.

She scrubbed her hands over her face; she looked a lot more plain without all the diamonds and her hair down and in tangles, although she hadn't bothered to take off her makeup, making her look like an angry raccoon. "Sorry. I'm so tired and jet-lagged. Don't go. My parents were horrible to you and I think I was too, and I'm sorry for that. They are terrible snots at the best of times, let alone at one a.m. or whatever time it was that we barged in here last night."

"It was after two," I corrected.

She exhaled and looked up at me. "Two. I'm sorry. They were on my last nerve and I'm sure I came across like a horrible witch. I assure you, I'm not one, though I can't say the same for my mother. Can we please start again?" she gave me a weak smile. "I'm Emmeline. Emmie to my friends, and I'd really like it if we were roommates. Please, please disregard my parents' rudeness."

"But you could have a private room," I said, suddenly wondering if I hadn't dreamed some of last night's conversation.

"Yes, but I don't want one. I want to be a normal girl here. Well," she gave me a goofy grin. "As normal as any of us are."

I gave her a smile. "Really? So I don't have to pack?"

She shook her head. "Not for many months."

I dropped back down onto my bed. "Thank God. It was a big enough job getting unpacked."

Emmeline—Emmie—smiled and nodded toward her luggage. "That's my job for today. I'm still exhausted but kind of

38

wired; I'm still on France time. And based on your accent, you sound like you know what I'm talking about."

I nodded. "Yes, but I've been in the States for a few days visiting my grandmother before I came to Rosewood. My parents are still back in London, but we're originally from here."

"I wish my parents could have sent me on my own," she said, stretching her arms above her head until I heard one of her shoulders crack. "But they like to visit their investment at least once a year." She ended her stretch and did air quotes around the word *investment.*

I frowned. "They consider you an investment?"

"Hardly," she said, laughing. "The Somerville library is their contribution to the school. It's the big red building in the back; a bunch of classrooms and a new library. They like to throw their money around and Mom attended here, so..." she waved her arm, not bothering to finish her sentence.

"What do your parents do?" I asked. They had to do something impressive to have funded their own building on campus.

She shrugged, "Fossil fuels mostly. You know, dig-up-dead-dinosaurs-and-kill-the-earth stuff." She looked around the room obviously finished with that topic of conversation. "I guess I should start unpacking, although all I want to do is go back to bed."

"Won't they give you a break today since you just got in?" *And you're a VIP,* I thought, but kept to myself.

She shook her head and stood up, stretching again, taking a few steps on her tiptoes. "I don't want a break. I want to be like everyone else." She combed her fingers through her hair and cringed. "And I can't exactly let everyone see me like this, so I'd better get moving."

It was still early; breakfast wasn't until 8 and classes were starting late after our 9 a.m. welcome assembly with the dean, for this, our first day. "I can help you unpack," I offered.

Emmie's eyes lit up. "Really? You'd do that for me after how heinous my parents were to you last night?"

Smiling at her, I said, "Sure. I may be new around here, but your parents aren't my roommates and from what I hear, Rosewoods look after each other."

Emmie smiled back. "You are shockingly nice. Thank you."

But what turned out to be shocking between us had absolutely nothing to do with me.

Emmeline Reinvented

Emmie pushed me toward the bathroom, telling me she needed a few minutes to wake up and get herself sorted, so I may as well shower and get ready for my day. Not needing extra encouragement to take a hot shower, I left her to it and enjoyed a nice long one, washing off the sleep and some of the stress over starting at a new school.

So far, Rosewood was turning out okay—the room mix-up had been solved quickly, the food had been good at dinner the night before (Celia had said with all the wealthy families, they couldn't get away with anything less than a five star chef) and all the girls I'd met so far were really nice.

And then there was Will. As I dried my hair, I allowed myself to think about him and wondered when I'd get to see him again. Chelly had said we'd have lots of opportunities to see the Westwood boys, but when?

I smirked at myself in the mirror; I was a little obsessed maybe, having met the guy once and already smitten. But that smile, the blue eyes, the cut of his angular face, not to mention his sense of humor and the attention he gave me. Who wouldn't be?

Although, if I was being honest, Evan, or *Jenks*, as Will had called him, was pretty fine, too. I normally wasn't into gingers, but he was a cross between Prince Harry and that actor, Michael Fassbender, and with his dry sense of humor, he came in a close second and if Will turned out not to be interested or available, I wouldn't be overly disappointed with him as a boyfriend.

And then there was the guy at the stables, Brady. He was enough to make a girl swoon with his dark hair and amber eyes. And that he loved horses was just an added bonus. But he was probably off limits; I figured staff weren't allowed to date students, even though he seemed really young.

"Right, Brooklyn," I said aloud to my reflection. "The new girl just walks in and gets her choice of cute guy." Doubtful. Evan and Will probably had not given me another thought after they dropped me and my trunk at Celia's room. And Brady probably just wanted to humor me and get me out of the stables so he could go home.

I finished up with my hair and started in on makeup turning my thoughts to more productive things, like worrying about my first day of classes.

A few minutes later, when I was finished, I stepped out into my bedroom to find I'd changed roommates again.

~ ♥ ~

There was a girl sitting at Emmie's desk, facing away from me. I couldn't see her face, but it couldn't be Emmeline with her long blond hair — this girl had short hair.

I looked around the corner to see if Emmie was in the closet, putting stuff away, but no. I looked back at the girl. She had a pixie cut that didn't even cover her neck. Well, it did, in places, but to be frank, it looked like she'd pulled it all into a ponytail and hacked it off.

But as she turned around to face me, I realized that's *exactly* what she had done. It *was* Emmeline.

"What have you done?" I gasped, my hands lifting to my mouth involuntarily. I mean, this girl didn't seem manic, but what else would make her cut her hair like that?

She was smiling as she ran her fingers through her hair, making it stand up. "I cut off my hair. What do you think?"

I think you're nuts. "Why?" I asked, not answering her question out loud.

She shrugged. "I do it every fall."

I looked around. "Without a mirror?"

"Well no, not usually, but I'll tidy it up now that you're out of the bathroom." She was obviously amused by my disbelief. "It's just hair. My parents freak out about it short, so I let it grow

42

for the summer, but I can't stand it and was dying to get rid of it. I couldn't wait one second longer."

Obviously. But it was unbelievable. This girl probably had more money than God and instead of going to a proper stylist, she lopped off her hair and, I realized with a glance to the wastepaper basket in the corner, threw it out like it was an empty Doritos bag.

She followed my glance and winced. "I know, it's wasteful, but it wasn't long enough to donate. I'll start growing it out earlier this year so it gets long enough."

"Huh?" I asked.

"For wigs. You know, for cancer patients. It has to be a certain length or they can't use it."

I just stared at the crazy girl in front of me.

She smiled back. "What?" she said, looking suddenly shy.

I shook my head. "You're brilliant, that's all."

She jumped up from her chair and gave me a big hug. "We're going to get along just great."

I opened my mouth to say something, but her cell beeped and she pulled away.

"A text from Dave, my boyfriend. He's anxious to see me — we haven't been together since last spring."

"Since you left for France?" I asked.

She glanced down at her phone and started pressing keys. "No, since I left here at the end of the school year. He goes to Westwood. That's the boys' school." She stopped texting and looked up at me and waggled her eyebrows. "Where you'll find *your* next boyfriend."

I laughed. It was like she'd read my mind.

"Unless you already have a boyfriend and are doing the long-distance thing."

"London is more long distance than I could handle," I said. She didn't need to know I never had a boyfriend in London.

"Right you are. Well, don't you worry. There are a ton of guys to choose from at Westwood."

Her phone beeped again. She rolled her eyes and looked

down. "Patience, young man. You will see me soon, I promise."

But I could tell by the way she grinned at her phone, Emmie was just as eager to see her boyfriend as he was to see her.

"How long have you been going out?"

"We hooked up after the Christmas dance last year."

"Sounds serious," I said.

She looked up, "I guess so. It feels weird, you know; it's been so long since we've seen each other. We've Skyped and stuff, but it's not the same. I miss smelling him and touching him; I just hope it's the same as it was."

I thought about Will and how good he'd smelled the day before, his mixture of subtle cologne and clean sweat.

"I met a guy yesterday," I said, feeling stupid even mentioning it.

"From Westwood?"

I nodded. "He helped me move in. Not that I think I really have a chance with him, but still."

"What are you talking about? Don't have a chance with him?" She gave me an obvious once-over. "You're plenty doable."

"Thanks," I said with a laugh.

"Okay, so I'm going to get ready real quick and then start unpacking and you can tell me all about this boy you met. I probably know him if he's not a freshman." She glanced at her luggage and exhaled, her shoulders dropping. "You still sure you want to help?"

I looked at the alarm clock. "We have about a half an hour."

She cringed and heaved one of her huge suitcases onto her bed before unzipping it.

"You go," I said, waving her toward the bathroom. "If you don't mind me in your stuff, I can at least get it out and organized."

Jumping from foot to foot, she made her way into the bathroom, "Thank you!" she yelled as she shut the door. "I really have to pee!"

That made me laugh, but I started pulling her stuff out of

her suitcase, folding it into neat piles. As I did, I wondered if Will and Dave were friends. Wouldn't that be convenient?

First Day of Classes

By the time Emmie was ready, we were just a few minutes from being due at breakfast. She came bursting out of the bathroom (her hair looking *très* cute and like it had been cut by a pro, I was relieved to see), saw the progress I'd made in putting her clothes away, gave me another quick hug and herded me out the door, claiming she was dying of starvation.

When we got to the dining hall, I fell into the background as she greeted the many girls who hadn't seen her since last spring. And I could tell that she was genuinely liked by many; I seemed to have hit the roommate jackpot.

Before we knew it though, it was time for morning announcements and then our assembly with the dean.

Even though I knew where the auditorium was, thanks to my tour the evening before, Emmie led me down the hall, chatting as we went.

"The dean's a dragon, but I guess I'm going to have to chat with her about this rooming situation," she sighed. "I'm sure my mother left a message on her voicemail before they even left the premises last night."

I wasn't surprised; her mother was totally the type. "What are you going to tell the dean?"

Emmie glanced over, a sheepish look making her look adorable under her pixie cut. "The same thing I do every year: that I want to be treated like every other girl here and if she doesn't like it, I would be just as happy to go to a public school where everyone is treated the same and parents don't donate buildings."

"Scandalous!" I said with a gasp and a dramatic palm pressed to my chest. But I appreciated her moxie. Though... "Would your parents ever let you go to a public school?"

She laughed. "Not in a million years. And believe me, I've

tried. I would rather their money go to something truly good, like building wells in third world countries or AIDS supports in Africa, but they want no part of it. They grew up in the age of *Dynasty* and love to be ostentatious and disgusting and spend their money on ridiculous things keeping up with the Joneses."

I didn't mention the diamonds she'd been wearing the night before could probably go a long way toward funding a third world well-digging project; maybe they were a gift or something.

"Anyway, like I said, the dean is a dragon, but with this she'll leave off and it's not a big deal. It's actually easier for them that I'm *not* demanding like my parents; I just need to reassure her it's not a problem where I am." She looked over at me. "I don't mean it that way—not that you're a problem. Oh you know what I mean."

I did and waved her off with a smile.

"So what do your parents do?" she asked. It was a simple enough question, but one I couldn't answer honestly. I hated lying to people, but by now it was a regular enough occurrence that I was able to let the lies roll off my tongue.

"They're both professors. Mom teaches English and my father is a professor of mathematics. They're both on sabbatical—she's studying at Oxford, which is why we were in London." Part of it was true in that Mom was studying at Oxford part-time and used to teach English before she quit her job to follow Dad around on assignment. Without a job, she attended classes and accumulated more degrees, which I guess is as good a way to keep busy as any.

It seemed to satisfy Emmie, anyway, which wasn't surprising—it was a boring enough story to discourage more questions.

We stepped inside the auditorium then, hit by a wall of voices as the girls awaited the call to order. "Where should we sit?" I asked.

Emmie scanned the crowd and then nodded toward the front. "Down there; Kaylee's got seats for us."

We made our way down the aisle and excused ourselves past a bunch of girls, me going first and trying not to bash into anyone. I smiled and nodded at the girls as I shuffled past, while Emmie greeted the ones she knew.

We finally got to our seats and settled in, Emmie on one side of me, Kaylee on the other. Celia was nowhere to be found, but as the dean walked up the few steps to the stage, Chelly came rushing in and plunked herself down beside Emmie.

"Hi," She huffed out, breathless.

The dean called everyone to order and the dull roar in the room lowered to a buzz and then just a few whispers as she scanned the crowd pointedly.

Finally, everyone quieted down and she began.

Sure, I was interested in getting good marks, but after three sentences the dean lost me and pretty much everyone else in the hall. You'd think after however many years doing this, she'd clue in. But maybe it was the respectful silence that made her think people were paying attention, when really, as I looked around, it was obvious everyone was just texting.

Including Emmie beside me. I nudged her with my elbow.

She tilted her head so she could give me a look, sticking the tip of her tongue through her lips.

I gave her a disapproving look back.

She angled the screen at me showing me she was texting Dave, as justification for blowing off the dean. Not that the bar was high.

Mss you. Can't wait to c u. was his last text.

Awwww, I mouthed. How sweet.

Emmie grinned and texted back while I watched over her shoulder: *2nite behind the stables at 8*

I looked up at her, eyes wide. I wasn't sure of all the Rosewood rules yet, but I had a feeling sneaking out of the dorms to meet guys was against at least one or five of them.

Not that Emmie cared, obviously; she rolled her eyes and continued typing with her thumbs.

I turned back to the front of the room, since reading her texts might be a bit creepy, when Kaylee grabbed my arm and squeezed. When I looked at her, she nodded toward the right side of the auditorium at the front. I glanced over, my eyes scanning the faculty, and then finally saw what she was looking at.

Mr. Stratton, the new science teacher.

"Rowr," Kaylee purred under her breath and waggled her eyebrows. "I have a weakness for smart guys. I can't wait for science."

I giggled, but couldn't help but agree.

It was after lunch before I got to actually meet the new science teacher. After the dean's hour-long blah-blah-academic-excellence-should-be-your-main-focus-but-you're-expected-to-be-a-good-Rosewood-citizen-blah-blah-blah speech, we filed out into the hall and parted ways.

Chelly and Emmie left for History class and Kaylee, Celia and I headed out to English Lit, which, based on the syllabus, was going to be a joke after everything I'd studied in London and had absorbed from Mom over the years. But with Kaylee and Celia in the class and a young, cool teacher, Ms. Ito, it was going to be fun and a no-brainer. My favorite kind of class!

Second was French, which was going to be another easy A, though I didn't know anyone there yet. And then Science, with the now infamous Mr. Stratton.

Kaylee and I sat together as lab partners, which I appreciated; I was starting to think, of all the girls I'd met so far, Kaylee and I might have the most in common, at least personality-wise. When it came to our backgrounds and families, she was the daughter of Hollywood producers, so she was really familiar with the celebrity life, where I was pretty much the opposite. But she was low-key and very focused on getting great marks so she could get into a pre-med program (she wanted no part of the famous life).

Not that the other girls didn't care about grades, but Kaylee was kind of a bookworm like me and we'd laughed when we compared notes and realized we'd both read all the required reading for the English Lit class well before the start of school.

And now we had another thing in common: our sudden interest in science.

"I don't know how I'm going to get any work done," Kaylee admitted as we watched Mr. Stratton come into the room, a soft-sided briefcase in one hand and a to-go cup in the other. He was wearing Dockers and a starched white button-down shirt kitted up with a tie under his blazer. His eyes were focused on his desk, like we didn't exist, although he must have heard all the excited whispering; it was almost deafening.

"Do you think he knows how attractive he is?" I asked Kaylee, my breath hitching as he took the blazer off and hung it over the back of his chair.

She smirked at me. "Only if he owns a mirror. Look at those shoulders."

I stifled a laugh and looked at him again. Now he had his briefcase on the desk and was taking out some papers, still ignoring the twenty girls in front of him who watched him like he was the main attraction at a zoo exhibit.

He took a sip of whatever he was drinking and put it down slowly, carefully on the corner of his desk.

The suspense was killing me.

Finally, he picked up a piece of paper, took a deep breath and looked up, his eyes sweeping across us, taking us in. His Adam's apple moved up and then down in his neck.

Kaylee whispered, "What do you want to bet this is his first teaching gig ever?"

Based on how young and nervous he looked, I wasn't about to take that bet.

"Good morning, ladies," he said after clearing his throat. "In case you weren't at dinner last night, I'm Mr. Stratton and I'm a new teacher here at Rosewood. I'm excited to be here and I'm sure we'll all learn a little something from each other over this term. Welcome."

Out of the corner of my eye, I saw Kaylee giggle at the 'Welcome'; we'd never be able to hear that word again without cracking up.

Luckily Mr. Stratton didn't notice and kept on with his little speech.

"...and to answer the question that I'm sure is at the forefront of all your minds, yes, this is my first teaching position and although they tell us in teachers' college never to admit that kind of vulnerability to students, I'm hoping here at Rosewood, you are mature and will use that information to go easy on me."

He pushed his thick-rimmed glasses up his nose and flashed us all one of those devastating smiles.

The class gave out a collected sigh.

Poor Mr. Stratton didn't stand a chance.

Community Service

My academic day finished out with P.E., which I'd looked forward to, since I'd thought it would mean a ride, but I was disappointed to find out that we didn't get an equestrian unit for a couple of weeks. Until then, we had our choice of football...er...*soccer* or archery.

Like every other girl I knew, I'd gone through a Katniss Everdeen stage so I'd already done some archery, and I felt like I needed something a bit more active to burn off some steam. I spent most of the period doing soccer drills with my classmates until I basically fell into a sweaty, exhausted heap; mission accomplished.

What I neglected to remember, though, was that at boarding school, your day isn't over after your last class; I still had dinner and the evening assembly to get through.

Dinner was fine (and after all that running around, I was starving) but then after that was the assembly about being a good Rosewood citizen. The dean was back at it again, telling us that part of Rosewood's mandate was to ensure we all became contributing members of our society.

"That's crap," Celia said under her breath as she leaned in close to me. "It's how they get free labor around here."

I gave her a look, hoping she'd explain, but she just waved toward the stage, like it would be obvious soon enough.

And it was, when the dean went on to explain that we would each find our assignments e-mailed to us at our special Rosewood e-mail addresses that had been issued to us and were on our schedules. Not having noticed it before, I pulled the folded up and dog-eared schedule out of my pocket and sure enough, at the top was my special Rosewood e-mail address.

She assured us that each of our assignments was hand-picked to fit in with our schedules and interests (Emmie, sitting on my other side, snorted here) and was non-negotiable except in very extreme circumstances.

"Death or…death," Celia said.

"If they really wanted us to contribute to society, they'd give us real volunteer opportunities," Emmie whispered. "They'd send us out in the community to do worthwhile things."

"So why don't they?" I asked.

Emmie shrugged. "Like Celia said, it's free labor. And also, they can't have us all scattered around outside the compound; too much of a security issue."

"Security?" I mean, I knew *I* might be a security issue, but what about the other kids?

Emmie leaned in closer. "Look around; there's a lot of money represented by all these kids. If some billionaire's kid gets kidnapped for a ransom, this school is screwed."

I wondered if Emmie was a 'billionaire's kid' as she continued. "Our parents pay for us to be safe here—that's a huge draw, right? I'm sure you saw the security booth at the front gate—and they can't exactly let us off campus to go be candy stripers or work on a big Habitat project with Joe Public."

She shook her head. "It makes sense, but it's still a waste of our talent and abilities. I could do a lot from here, organizing projects and fundraising online, but instead, they're going to make me work in the kitchen or something and call it 'community work' that's going to make me a better citizen. Right."

"As long as I don't get stuck shoveling crap in the stables again," Chelly said. "It's like they knew I hate horses and gave me the worst job in the world."

"I'd love to work in the stables," I said, suddenly eager to get back to our room so I could check my e-mail, figuring the new girl surely had to draw the short straw and get stuck mucking stalls.

Celia snorted. "If you *want* to work in the stables, you'll end up cleaning the giant oatmeal-encrusted pots at, like, five in the morning. That's just how it works here. And they never let anyone change—because then everyone would, right?"

Awesome. I couldn't wait.

~❤~

Emmie and I returned to our room after assembly to log into the Rosewood webmail and get our assignments. She sat on her bed, her laptop across her thighs while I sat at my desk, working on my tablet.

"How did *that* happen?" she exclaimed, incredulous, but as I glanced over at her, I couldn't tell if it was *good* incredulous or *bad* incredulous.

"What is it?" I asked, still trying to get logged in.

She looked up at me. "They put me in student services. School liaison."

"What does that mean?" I asked. I still couldn't tell if she was happy or not, but it sounded better than cleaning pots in the kitchen. At least she probably wouldn't have to get her hands dirty, although I had a feeling Emmie wouldn't mind physically digging into a project, as long as she was really helping people.

"It means I'll be working with my counterpart at Westwood to coordinate events: dances, outings, talent shows."

The slow smile that spread across her face told me this was a good thing. A very good thing.

She looked back down at her computer. "I told them no special treatment, but you know what? Screw it. I'm okay with this, if it's thanks to nepotism."

I wondered if juniors at public schools even know what *nepotism* means, but for girls at Rosewood, it was a way of life; kids get special treatment just because of who they're related to. Although to be special and stand out at Rosewood, you had to be the upper crust of the upper crust—like have a building donated by your parents.

"What did you get?" she asked, putting her laptop on her bedspread and scooting to the end of her bed to look over my shoulder.

54

I finally got into my e-mail and sifted through the several automated e-mails from the registrar's office about drop and pick, school policies, etc, etc, to find the one with the subject line, 'CSA: community service assignment'.

Holding my breath, I opened it and scanned for the word 'stables' or maybe 'equestrian center' but no. I read it from the beginning:

> *Dear **Ms. Prescott**, we are pleased to have you be a part of our award-winning community service program where you will give back to your community through volunteership that will help build skills that will last you a lifetime.*
>
> *Your assignment is located at: **The Rosewood Academy's state-of-the-art laundry facilities.***
>
> *Please report to your community service mentor: **Mr. Ammaturo***
>
> *At: **The Housekeeping office, Main building, Sub-basement B. Tomorrow at 7:00 p.m.***
>
> *After which, your scheduled hours of service will be: **Monday through Friday, 6:00 -7:30 a.m.***

The crack of dawn? And laundry? Really?

"Oh, that's unfortunate," Emmie said from behind me. "I don't know what you did to make the dean hate you, but that's pretty bad."

And it only got worse.

The Stables

Twenty minutes later, as I was going over the science syllabus, Emmie came out of the bathroom looking especially cute in her jeans and a sweater. She'd spiked her hair up a little and put on makeup, making her eyes pop. Although I hadn't met Dave, I had a feeling she was going to knock his socks off.

"You look awesome," I said as she opened her mouth, undoubtedly to ask what I thought.

Her mouth clamped shut and then she smiled and came over to give me a quick hug around my shoulders. "Thank you, Brooklyn. I'm soooo nervous to see him. I hope he still likes me."

"Have you lost your mind?" slipped from my lips, making her frown until I hastily added, "You are cute and nice and truly, *the* most down-to-earth person I've ever met. You feed the hungry, clothe the poor and cut your own hair—what's not to like?"

She smiled sweetly and I stood up out of my chair so I could give her a proper hug. I'd never made friends easily, nor had I ever been a touchy-feely type, but something about Emmie made me feel like I'd met my best friend soul mate.

"You only have one fault," I said into her ear as I squeezed her tight and then pushed away to look into her eyes. "Your ridiculous modesty. And even that's endearing." I rolled my eyes dramatically.

"You are the best," she said, glancing at my clock. "Shoot, is that the time? I need to run out to the stables; Dave's going to be waiting for me."

The stables! I'd completely forgotten to sign up for the equestrian team. I'd meant to go to the office after P.E. but after my shower, all I could focus on was dinner.

"I'll walk down with you," I said, hoping maybe they had a sign-up list that I could access after-hours.

We left the room and walked side by side down the hallway to the stairs. "Where are you off to?" Emmie asked.

"To the stables, also."

She screwed up her face. "Um. Three's a crowd, you know. Ha, ha." she said, her laugh not as breezy as I think she intended.

"What?" And then I remembered in that moment that we really didn't know each other that well and she might think...

"Oh, no!" I said, looking into her eyes, embarrassed that she'd think I'd make myself into a third wheel, and needing to set her straight. "I wasn't planning to come with you to see Dave. I need to go to the office at the stables so I can sign up for the equestrian team."

She stopped on the landing, halfway down the stairs, and looked at me for another second. Suddenly, her face broke into a smile and she rolled her eyes, shaking her head at the same time. "I'm so stupid. See? See how nervous I am?"

I waved her off and started down the stairs. "It's understandable. You haven't seen him in months. But I saw his texts; he's still into you. If anything, probably more than he was. You know what they say: absence makes the heart grow fonder."

Emmie nodded.

We got to the bottom of the stairs and I slid my arm around her. "After tonight, you'll be back to normal. You have nothing to worry about."

She started toward the door and noticed I wasn't following. "Aren't you coming?"

"No, you go. I need to make a stop first." Just so she knew I wasn't going to interrupt or make things any weirder for her and Dave.

"Okay, wish me luck," she said.

"You don't need luck, just go. It'll be fine," I said.

She ducked out the door and I turned the other way to head into the kitchen. Mealtimes were pretty structured, but there was something of a snack buffet that the girls told me was always stocked, 24-7. I grabbed two apples and a pear, putting them into the front pocket of my hoodie, and arranged a handful of carrot sticks onto a paper towel, rolling it up into a bundle and stuffing it into my pocket.

After a good five minutes of checking out the various types of coffee, sodas and snacks available, I was sure Emmie had enough time to get around to the back of the stable building where her boyfriend awaited her (which, I had to admit, was very romantic). I headed outside and made a beeline for the door, keeping my eyes straight ahead of me, so I wouldn't see any serendipitous PDAs if they weren't as hidden as they meant to be.

The door was unlocked again, so I figured someone was inside. I called out a "Hello?" but got no response, so I entered and turned down the hall toward the office.

One of the horses nickered, and I wondered if it was Sir Lancelot, looking to lure me into a bite. I chuckled, thinking of Brady's name for him: *Sir Bitesalot.*

"Sign up first, then I'll say hello," I muttered aloud to myself. As expected, the office door was locked up tight, but there was a sign-up form outside, complete with a pen on a string tacked next to it on the bulletin board.

"That's convenient," I said. But as I reached for the pen, I heard something: a voice.

And not a horse's nicker or grunt, either. It was a boy's voice followed by a girl's voice. He said something, she responded. Then she laughed. I turned my head toward the voices and realized they were outside.

Emmie and Dave.

They must have been right outside the back wall of the stables, just outside the office. I couldn't hear what they were saying, but they were obviously reconnecting after their months apart.

I was glad it was going well; Emmie was a really great

person and even though I'd just met her, she obviously deserved to have a good guy. A small part of me, the deep, dark part that I would never admit existed, was the tiniest, littlest bit jealous. Sure, not many girls got to go to super-exclusive boarding schools with stables and all the amenities of the rich and famous, but Emmie already *had* everything. Maybe it seemed like life was too easy for her.

And now that her and Dave were officially an item again, was that going to mean she wouldn't want to be friends with me?

I mean, I realized we'd just met, but I'd quickly gotten the impression that we were going to be super-close friends—we'd really seemed to connect.

Boys always make things more complicated.

Especially for the single friend.

Not that I wanted Dave to break up with her or anything—not at all. Just maybe, I admitted to myself, I wanted what they had for me, too. Was it too much to ask that a guy notice me and want to hook up with *me* behind the stables? Two years in London, surrounded by cute guys with British accents and I couldn't even get a guy to look my way at a school dance, let alone want to date me.

And really, what made me think it would be any different here? At least at my school in London, I'd had the benefit of being somewhat exotic: the American girl. But here, I was nothing but the new girl. At an all-girls' school.

There was a good chance I'd get to see Will at the dance, but would he be interested? Had he just flirted with me because I was the new girl and had that damsel in distress vibe going on? When I thought of all the other girls at Rosewood, I couldn't imagine he'd ever be interested in me. Assuming he was even single.

Tears pricked at the corners of my eyes, making me feel even more pathetic.

"Oh that's rich, Brooklyn," I said. "Now you're hosting a pity-party for one in the stables, where even the horses don't care. Ugh. Nice way to make a fresh start."

As I stood there, berating myself, Emmie and Dave's voices got quieter and lower and they seemed to be talking more slowly. Then they stopped altogether. Before I even realized what I was doing, I was straining my ears to hear more. I was suddenly rewarded with the softest of moans.

Oh my God; they're making out! Not that it should have surprised me, but what *was* most surprising (and horrifying), was that I was standing there, *eavesdropping*.

Suddenly feeling like a total perv and the worst friend imaginable, I shook my head, mentally shut my ears and turned my attention to the top of the sign up form so I could get my name on it and get out of earshot:

Equestrian Team -
Tryouts this Friday, 7:00 a.m. in the indoor arena.
Must be available for practice M-F 6:30 a.m – 8:00 a.m.
& Sundays 7:00 a.m. - 12:00 p.m.
Sign up - one (1) name per slot below:

I blinked and read it again. Seven a.m.: right in the middle of my Community Service assignment. The one that was non-negotiable and unchangeable.

"Seriously?"

I took a deep breath and read the form a third time, hoping it would change as I read it. Or maybe I'd read it wrong the first two times.

But no.

Everything hit me in that moment and I was suddenly desperately homesick. Even though I didn't have anywhere that I really called home anymore, I missed my parents and my brother and the comfort of everything going the way I expected it to, even if it wasn't the life I really wanted. At least it was comfortable and easy and I never got my hopes squashed by a dragon of a dean who I'd never met but who seemed to hate me anyway.

Yep, definitely a pity party, I thought.

I sniffled and wiped my eyes on the cuff of my hoodie.

"Pathetic," I muttered.

"What's pathetic?" I heard from behind me, startling me.

I spun around on Brady, pressing my palm to my chest to try to ease my racing heart. "Stop doing that!"

Wearing a navy and green flannel shirt and what appeared to be his signature jeans, he held up his hands in the universal symbol for '*what did I do?*'

"You scared me half to death," I explained.

He gave me a wide-eyed look. "I could say the same of you. I come in here to lock up and here you are, lurking around. For the second time, I might add."

"I'm not lurking," I said, stuffing my hands into my hoodie pockets, reminded of the fruit I'd brought for the horses.

Brady's eyes glanced down at my belly and he nodded at it. "Are those billiard balls in there or are you happy to see me?"

My face heated up instantly and I'm sure it burned a delightful crimson at his not-so-innocent joke. In answer, I pulled out an apple. "For the horses," I choked out.

Smooth, Brooklyn.

He gave me a knowing grin and then the smile dissolved as he looked closer, stepping toward me. I began to fidget as it suddenly felt like he was looking right through me. "Hey. Are you okay?"

My first instinct was to nod and wave him off. But apparently he'd asked the perfect question to unlock my mouth, and then words just started falling out.

"No. I'm not okay." I said, jerking my thumb toward the bulletin board. "I just went to sign up for the team and found out the practices are at the same time as my stupid community service assignment. I won't be able to join after all. And of course, it's the one thing at this school I was actually looking forward to."

61

Then, because my display wasn't pathetic enough, tears eked out of my eyes, rolling down my face and I could do nothing to stop them but swipe at them with my hoodie sleeve. Embarrassed, I dropped my head, staring at my shoes, unable to bring myself to look at Brady. I was probably doing him a favor, since he was probably calculating the path of least resistance to get away from me.

"Hey, hey," he said, from right in front of me, making my head snap up toward him. His stunning amber eyes were intent on mine, concerned.

He reached out as though to touch my shoulder, but hesitated and dropped his arm, shoving his hand into his jeans pocket instead. "It's okay. You can fix this."

I shook my head. "I don't think so. My friends said the dean never lets people change their assignments, no matter what."

"No matter what?" he asked.

"That's what they said." I wasn't about to tell him their exact words. Or that Emmie'd called her a dragon; she was Brady's employer, after all.

"She can be a bit...rigid," he admitted, the right corner of his mouth twitching up into a tiny smile.

"That's diplomatic," I said.

"Generous," he replied, with a snort.

"I've heard she's a dragon," I blurted out. And then gasped. So much for not trashing his employer. "Sorry!"

Brady barked out a laugh. "No, don't apologize. She definitely has dragon-like properties."

I felt stupid, but he didn't seem to mind. "Why don't you sign up," he said, pointing at the form.

I frowned. "I told you, my assignment..." I broke off because he was shaking his head. "What?"

"I'm sure there's a way around it."

I stared at him. If there was a way around it, it wasn't coming to me, especially with his eyes so focused on mine. Unwavering. Making me blush again for no reason.

Swallowing, I turned away, looking at the paper on the wall.

"Do you think Coach Fleming would talk to her?"

"He might."

I looked back at him. "Really?"

He shrugged. "He's always looking for good candidates for the team. Especially dressage. And," he paused to look around, like he was about to tell me a grave secret. My heart stuttered as he leaned closer, filling my nose with his masculine smell: fifty percent boy, fifty percent tack, one-hundred percent amazing.

He was almost close enough to kiss me, and as if they were hoping it would happen, my eyes drifted down to his mouth. Involuntarily, I leaned forward.

He cleared his throat, snapping my attention back up to his eyes.

"I have it on good authority that the dean has a soft spot for dressage. We've had a sub-par team for years, but if we had someone with four blue..."

"Five," I said, interrupting him. "I have five blue ribbons." Which was true, but probably wasn't a good indicator of my skill as much as the lack of skill in anyone else at my old stables.

He nodded, "Five. Like I said: impressive. Leave it with me; I'll see what I can do."

I opened my mouth to thank him, when I heard Emmie's laugh, muffled, but loud enough that Brady would be able to hear it if he was paying attention. One glance at his face told me he hadn't heard, but it was just a matter of time if we stuck around.

I cleared my throat loudly. "So I have all this fruit and carrots. Can I give it to the horses?"

He pointed at the form again. "Sign up."

"Right." I cleared my throat again while I scribbled my name on the form, cursing the pen that decided it didn't want to write upright. I pretty much scratched my name through the page and quickly turned back to Brady.

"Okay, good to go." I cleared my throat again to cover Emmie's giggle. "Sorry. Something in my throat."

He gave me a weird sideways look, but didn't say anything

more as he led me away from the office and down the hall towards the stalls.

"So, do you ride?" I asked him. It felt like a stupid question; asking the stable boy if he rode, but you never know. And anyway, it filled the weird silence that was stretching between us.

He gave me a look, his right eyebrow raised.

"What?" I asked. "Did I say something wrong?" I suddenly had a panic attack that he had fallen from a horse and had some sort of PTSD or something.

He shook his head and grinned. "No. Nothing's wrong. Yes, I ride a little. Come on, let's distribute your goodies and then I have to lock up. As much as I'd like to hang out here all night with you, I do have an early day tomorrow."

My heart fluttered in my chest at his words. Was Brady flirting with me? No, he was staff here and that had to be against the rules, even if he did seem kind of young; he was probably older than he looked, anyway.

Probably he was just being nice to the new girl who'd cried on his shoulder over her childish problems.

Yes, that had to be it. But why didn't my pounding heart believe it?

Love Rekindled

"I don't know what I was nervous about, but you were right, Brooklyn: it was fine. No. It was *better* than fine, it was amazing! Dave is amazing."

It was the sixth time Emmie'd used the word *amazing* since she'd returned from her stables rendezvous, kicked off her shoes and threw herself onto her bed, almost two and a half minutes before. It was tempting to point out that she was going to qualify for the 'overused word drinking game' if she wasn't careful, but her excitement was infectious, so I just let her ride it out. Realizing I wasn't going to get back to reading my textbook anytime soon, I wondered if I'd get any work done this year with Emmie as my roommate. I might have to figure out somewhere else to study for exams, but for now, before the workload got too heavy, I didn't mind.

And I loved her energy; I hoped maybe some would wear off on me.

She bounced a little on her bed. "He looks even better than I remembered, since his hair's grown out. I mean, you just can't see it on Skype, you know? And it's so soft and he smells exactly how I remembered; clean and masculine and kind of like leather and just pure goodness, you know?"

I nodded, getting the feeling if I opened my mouth, she'd just talk over me anyway.

"And the kissing," she said, fluttering her lashes, her fingers rising to touch her lips. My face heated up as I guiltily remembered hearing them making out, but she didn't seem to notice and went on. "He is such a good kisser. I think I may have missed that more than anything else. Although, the talking was nice. Not that we talked about much of anything." She giggled sheepishly. "But hearing his voice first hand while he was touching me..." she trailed off, all swoony.

"So, you're breaking up then?" I asked, joking.

She rolled her eyes. "Of course. I'm pretty much done with him; you can have him next."

I laughed, but didn't say anything. I mean, Dave sounded perfect; nice and good-smelling and of course, the good kisser part, but secretly, I was still thinking about Will.

"And, the best part? I'm going to get to work with him through my CSA—he's doing school liaison, too. How lucky is that?"

I wasn't sure luck had much to do with it, but I was happy for her and hoped that if I ever got a boyfriend, that she'd be happy for me if we got extra opportunities to be together.

"Oh no!" she said suddenly. "Wait! *Your* guy. I completely forgot to ask about him." It was like she'd been reading my mind, or maybe I had a neon sign on my face or something.

But compared to her real relationship, my little flirtation with Will seemed stupid and insignificant now, at least out loud. I waved her off. "It's no big deal. He was just a cute guy who helped me with my luggage, that's all. I'm sure it was nothing." Because it was going to amount to nothing, if my past history with guys was any sort of indicator. But he *had* smelled good, and his hair looked soft and I would have loved to have found out if he was a good kisser, too.

She gave me a look. "What? What's going on with you?"

I avoided her eyes, smoothing out my bedspread over my legs and picking at the corner of the textbook I'd put down when she'd burst into the room. "Nothing."

"What happened at the stables? You seem...I don't know, different."

I told her about the equestrian team conflict, but when I was done, she frowned at me.

"What?" I asked.

"That's not it," she said. "Something...you're unsettled or something."

Even though I'd been thinking about Will, Emmie made me think about Brady back at the stables and how he'd made me feel exactly that: unsettled. "It's nothing."

Emmie got up off her bed and sat down on mine, digging her legs under the covers and poking me with her toes. "It's not nothing. I'm very intuitive and I'm never wrong." She studied my face, making me blush under her scrutiny.

"Was there a boy there?"

My face got even hotter.

"Well that answers it," she declared with a snort, nudging me with her foot again. Her eyes went suddenly wide. "Wait. It was him, wasn't it? The trunk mover! What happened?"

I knew I wasn't getting away from the interrogation, so I figured best to just tell her and get it over with.

"No. It wasn't him.   It was the stable guy. Brady." I shrugged. "We're friends, I guess. We met last night when I went out to hang out with the horses. But it's nothing." I thought about him standing so close to me and how it had almost felt like he'd been about to kiss me. But it had to have been just my imagination, and I wasn't about to make myself look like an idiot by saying something about it to Emmie.

She stared at me and blinked three times. "Brady?"

"Yes, Brady." Dread washed over me at her expression. She must have thought I was into him or something. "But of course he's staff and obviously older; it's not like *that*. We're just friends. He said he was going to talk to the coach about getting me on the team and getting my community service assignment changed. And I just met him. Like I said, it's not like that..." I clamped my mouth shut, realizing I was babbling like a crazy person who might be overcompensating for something that she wasn't willing to admit to her roommate or herself.

Emmie closed her eyes and shook her head for several moments. Frowning, and with her eyes still closed, she said, "Wait, *what*? He was going to talk to *what* coach?"

All that kissing must have scrambled her brain, I thought, wondering if I wasn't speaking clearly. "The equestrian coach: Fleming. Brady said he would talk to him about getting me on the team and seeing if the dean would change my community service assignment."

She opened her eyes and looked straight into mine. "Brooklyn," she said, looking at me as though I was daft. "First of all, the dean changes community service assignments for NO ONE. Ever. And secondly, and, I think, most importantly, so pay attention: Brady *is* Coach Fleming."

My brain seemed to stall out for a moment, but when her words started to make sense, I did a double-take. "What? No. He's older than us, but he's too young to be a coach."

Emmie put her hands on my cheeks and held my head in place, inches from hers, when she said, very slowly, "Brady Fleming is our equestrian coach. He attends Westwood as a student and works here part time in the stables and teaching equestrian. He's going to the next Olympics."

"Olympics?" I croaked.

She nodded, not letting go of my face. "Yes. The Olympics. You know, that sport event thing that happens, I don't know, every four years or so. It's kind of a big deal?"

"He's going to the Olympics," I repeated. "In what?"

"Dressage."

Of course. That makes all the sense in the world. "If he's going to the Olympics, why is he working here at Rosewood?"

She shrugged. "He goes to Westwood on an athletic scholarship. I imagine going to the Olympics isn't free, neither is training or paying for a horse and vet bills and all that."

It took a moment for this all to sink in. And then I remembered, "Oh. My. God!" I looked at her. "Emmie!"

"What?" she asked, but she was laughing. I could hardly blame her; if it wasn't me who'd made a total fool of myself in front of our equestrian coach, I'd be laughing, too.

"I bragged about my stupid blue ribbons and even asked him if he rides at all. He must think I'm a total idiot. No wonder he gave me that look."

She let go of my face to laugh and throw her arms around my shoulders and give me a squeeze. "You are so cute. What did he say?"

I smirked, in spite of myself. "He said he rides *a little.*"

She snorted. "Ha! That's awesome. But more importantly," she dropped her voice and gave me a pointed look. "Isn't he delicious?"

"Emmie!"

Feigning shock, she suddenly let me go. "Oh come on. Tell me you didn't notice. He's beautiful and broody; what's not to like?"

"Broody?"

"Yes. Broody and moody, snarling all the time. Tortured. So hot."

I wasn't sure we were talking about the same guy. "I didn't get that from him."

"Tall guy, black hair, honey brown eyes?"

I nodded. Definitely Brady.

"Was he wearing tight pants? His best assets are below the belt."

"Emmie!" I exclaimed again, raising my palms to my hot cheeks.

She winked and got up out of my bed. "Relax, I meant his butt and thighs from all that horseback riding. You have such a dirty mind, Brooklyn Prescott." She gave me a wave over her shoulder. "I don't think you're as innocent as you let on."

Indeed I was, but her comment was rhetorical, so I didn't respond. And anyway, by the time I would have thought of something to say, she had taken her pajamas into the bathroom and shut the door behind her.

But as I sat there, still stunned from learning Brady was actually the equestrian instructor, something nagged at me. Why hadn't he told me? He'd had several opportunities: when I first met him and then again tonight. And it couldn't be an oversight—he'd said he would talk to Coach Fleming on my behalf. He could have come clean right then. So much for us being friends as I'd thought.

So much for me liking Coach Fleming as he'd said I would.

He had intentionally deceived me. But why?

The Dean

The next day I was in French class, easily conjugating verbs about ten minutes before the bell was to ring, when I got called to the dean's office. My heart pounded in my chest and the girls around me started whispering, but I couldn't be in trouble already, could I? I was the good girl. And I'd just gotten to Rosewood.

Then I realized maybe it was about the equestrian team. Maybe, despite his little deception, Brady—Coach Fleming—had followed through on his promise to get me on the team.

Nervous, I packed up my things and left the classroom, pulling the dog-eared campus map from my backpack to find the dean's office.

Once I got there, I realized it was exactly what I would have expected the office of the dean of students of a very exclusive girls' school to be: all rich wood and ceiling-high shelves of books, many leather-bound. There was a large but utilitarian wood desk placed strategically in front of the ornately carved door with a plaque that read "Dean Haywood". Sitting at the desk was a bespectacled secretary. As my eyes landed on her, I startled a little; she was staring at me over the top of her reading glasses.

The entire scene was so cliché, I almost laughed.

Almost.

"Um, hi. I'm Brooklyn Prescott," I said. "Here to see the dean."

The woman pointed at a chair behind me against the wall. "Sit. I'll let her know you're here, Ms. Prescott."

The secretary didn't move or pick up a phone, but turned her gaze to her computer screen and I figured in today's day and age, she must have e-mailed or IMed her.

Several minutes later, long enough for me to consider

starting to bite my nails again, the brass doorknob turned. I held my breath as the dean came out.

She looked a lot taller here in her office than she had on the stage, speaking from the podium. She wore a well-tailored suit, maybe Chanel, and her silver hair was wound around her head in a complicated twist that looked like it was compiled from a long braid. If I had to guess, she had hair midway down her back, but chose to pile it up on top of her head. Why bother? I wondered.

"Ms. Prescott," she said, her eyes landing on me, her expression unreadable. "Come in."

I took a deep breath as I stood up and hooked my backpack over my right shoulder, following her back into her office.

"The door, please," she said, although it sounded a lot more like a demand than a request. I carefully shut the heavy door behind me and came to stand at the desk, not daring to sit down until told to.

She took a seat in her large leather chair and leaned forward, her elbows on the blotter as she steepled her fingers. She did not invite me to sit. "Coach Fleming came to see me today."

"Yes, ma'am," I said because she'd stopped talking and seemed to be expecting something from me.

"He tells me you want to join the equestrian team."

"That's correct, ma'am." I shifted my weight from one foot to the other and glanced at the two chairs in front of me. Had she forgotten they were there? *What do I do now?* It felt so awkward to stand there, but she hadn't said anything, so I stayed where I was.

"I'm to understand that you've won over a dozen blue ribbons in dressage."

Over a dozen? That was a stretch. But I had no way of knowing who was exaggerating, and wasn't about to call her on it. "I was very successful," I said, figuring that was enough of the truth. "I worked very hard."

She inclined her head slightly; respect, perhaps?

"He also tells me that the practice schedule conflicts with

your community service assignment."

I nodded.

"What do you intend to do about that?"

What do *I* intend to do? Huh?

"I'm sorry, ma'am. I don't understand."

She leaned back in her chair and crossed her arms over her chest. "You can't be at two places at once, unless I'm more behind on reading my scientific journals than I thought. So how are you going to handle this situation?"

"I...I had hoped maybe you could excuse me from my community service assignment?"

When the dean laughed humorlessly, I knew I'd said the wrong answer.

"Try again, Ms. Prescott."

I opened my mouth, but nothing came out.

"Let me give you a hint, young lady," she said, smirking. But not in an evil way, just sort of like she was amused. Yes, I realize there's a fine line in this situation between amused and evil, but I didn't get the feeling that she was really *trying* to be a dragon, despite the outcome being that she was, well, being a dragon.

"Most of the girls here at Rosewood come from privilege, you included, of course, since you're not on scholarship. And with privilege often comes a sense of entitlement and the belief that anything can be bought or influenced to desired results. That may be true in some aspects of life, but not all, and I do you no favors if I make your life perfect. What we try to foster here is an appreciation for life being difficult and unfair and not always what we sign up for. There are consequences to our actions and nothing we do is ever in a vacuum. Do you understand me?"

Sort of. "You're saying no one gets off easy here."

She nodded. "In essence, yes."

"So you're not going to let me get out of the community service assignment."

"That is correct," she said, leaning forward again, resting her forearms on the desk. She continued to stare at me, waiting.

I cleared my throat. "Ma'am, would you please provide me with a different assignment? One that is at a different time, so I may attend the equestrian practices?"

"No."

What?

"Ma'am, I'm not trying to get out of doing an assignment, but if you could..."

"Stop!" She slapped her hand down on the desk blotter, halting me mid-sentence and almost making me pee my pants. She exhaled loudly and then continued, thankfully in a more reasonable tone. "Ms. Prescott, I understand your predicament, but I am not going to do anything to make this easy for you. I can't change things for every girl who comes in here and wants to adjust her schedule, can I?"

"No, ma'am."

"So. What are *you* going to do?"

Besides wish I'd ditched French? "Um, not join the equestrian team?"

She frowned, looking disappointed, almost making me burst into tears on the spot.

"Is that truly your only option?"

I swallowed as I stood there, fidgeting from foot to foot and trying desperately to figure out what she wanted from me. But maybe...maybe what she wanted from me is exactly what she was saying: that she wanted me to figure it out, find a solution on my own.

But what? Shifting my weight again, I looked around the room as though her diploma-covered walls would offer up suggestions.

Sadly, they didn't.

"Ms. Prescott?"

I looked at the dean again.

"I'm a very busy woman. I am responsible for this entire school and all of the pupils and staff in it. Are you wasting my time?"

"No ma'am," I said, but feared it was a lie. She continued to stare at me, her eyes unwavering.

She opened her mouth and I was sure she was about to throw me out when I said, "Wait! Would it be acceptable if I could trade assignments with one of my fellow students?"

The smallest of smiles tugged at the corners of her mouth. "If you were able to find a student to trade assignments with, under these circumstances and this one time, I would find that acceptable and allow it so you could join the equestrian team. However," she gave me a pointed look, "If I find out that you used any sort of negative coercion or threats, you will be off that team in a heartbeat. Do you understand me?"

My heart danced in my chest. I was going to get to join the team! "Yes, ma'am," I said, managing to keep my excitement in check.

"However…"

Ugh. Why is there *always* a however?

"Since Mr. Fleming assures me of your advanced equestrian skills, negating the need for a tryout, you will report today to your assignment as directed and will continue with it until such time as you find a replacement. When you do find a replacement, you must return here and give my secretary a letter signed by both of you agreeing to the change. Just because I allowed you this, doesn't mean you get a free pass. Understand?"

"Yes, ma'am," I said. "Thank you."

She gave one of her little nods. "You are welcome. Dismissed."

I bowed a little and turned toward the door.

"Oh and Ms. Prescott?"

I turned.

"What is your current assignment?"

"Laundry."

With a wide-eyed stare that I was unable to interpret, she wished me the best of luck.

~♥~

It didn't take long to figure out the dean was being facetious when she'd wished me luck finding someone to take my community service assignment.

Chelly and Celia were both somewhat sympathetic in their denials, which were swift and about what I expected. Kaylee did seem sorry, but she'd just signed up for morning yoga at the sports complex and Emmie, well, I didn't even ask her since she had such a plum assignment with her boyfriend.

So then I had to start asking strangers. Not a great plan, but what else could I do? Although, now that it had become what seemed like an impossible task, I was starting to wonder if it was even worth it. Did I really want to join the equestrian team so badly? Did I want to end up spending so much time with Brady, who had intentionally deceived me?

I had half a mind to go out to the stables to confront him about it, but first I had to report to Sub-basement B for my first laundry shift.

Which explained exactly why I was never going to find anyone to take my assignment.

Friendship

That night, I returned from my orientation in the laundry and wanted nothing more than to fall into bed, but I had what felt like eight layers of dried sweat, bleach, detergent and other people's grime all over me.

"Orientation" had turned into two hours of hard labor, sorting all the laundry; sheets, towels, table linens and loads of personal clothes, putting it into the massive machines and then sorting everything as it came out again. I couldn't believe there was so much to wash already after only a couple days on campus, but one of the full-time employees told me that most of the staff and some teachers worked year round. That meant this was just a fraction of what I was to expect starting the following week. Awesome.

I really needed to switch assignments—forget about how much I wanted to join the equestrian team, if I continued in this job, it might just kill me. The only saving grace was that it would only be an hour and a half a day, although I couldn't imagine doing a full day of school after all this physical work. I wasn't in the best shape ever, but still, this assignment was beyond hard core.

So when I got into my room, I was desperate for a shower and then bed. Thankfully Emmie was out, since I was so tired, coherent speech wasn't possible. Kicking off my shoes at the door, I tore off my clothes right there and headed straight into the bathroom. I stepped into the tub, turning on the shower, bathing on autopilot.

When I emerged, the room was still quiet, but it was different than it had been before dinner. It took me a moment to realize Emmie'd been up to some decorating while I'd been out; her side of the room was covered in posters. Most were for PETA (thankfully no gory ones), Fair Trade and other human service organizations. Except for the one beside her pillow that was for a tatted up punk band.

If I hadn't been a comatose zombie, I would have found that amusing. But all I had the brain to do was set my alarm for 5:45, because I was due back at the laundry at 6:00.

FML.

~ ♥ ~

Something dragged me out of a dead sleep. One of those really deep sleeps that when you wake up, you have no idea where you are or whether it's morning or night. Or sometimes, who you are.

I looked around, but it was still dark, so I put my head back down.

"Brooklyn?"

I groaned.

"Wake up," Emmie whispered, which seemed counterproductive.

"What?" I moaned.

"We need to talk."

"In the middle of the night?" I didn't even care how whiny I sounded. She was being a very bad roommate.

"It's not even ten o'clock!"

"In the morning?" I suddenly sprang up to seated, squinting at her as she sat on the edge of my bed. The bathroom light was on, but it was so far away, all I could see was her shadow.

"No, silly. At night. It's like nine-forty. How long have you been back here?"

My upper body wasn't able to hold itself up anymore; I fell back onto my pillow. "I don't know. They let us leave the laundry at 9, but they just about killed me. What's going on?" I felt it necessary to ask. I didn't really care, but felt like I should.

"We need to talk," she said again, although this time I was slightly more conscious.

I couldn't see her face, but her tone suggested something

77

serious. I sat up again, more slowly this time. "What's the matter?"

She blew out a breath. I reached for my lamp and turned it on, blinking at the sudden light. "What is it, Emmie? Did something happen with Dave at your meeting tonight?"

"No, it's not that."

She was making me nervous. "What then?"

She exhaled again and then said, "Well, I know we don't know each other that well yet, but it's kind of like I feel like we really connected or something. Maybe even like we knew each other in past lives, if you buy into that kind of thing."

I didn't, but I had felt the connection. I nodded.

"Well," she looked down at her hands, fidgeting her fingers.

"What is it, Emmie?" The sooner she blurted out whatever it was, the sooner I could get back to sleep. Yes, now I was being the bad roommate, but I was *really* tired.

"Why didn't you ask me to trade CSAs with you?"

I had to have heard her wrong. "What?"

"You asked everyone else except me."

"Yeah. Because you have a plumb position with your boyfriend. I wouldn't ask you to change that."

"Why not?"

"Emmie, have you been drinking?"

She didn't laugh. "No, Brooklyn. I'm serious. Why?"

As a stalling tactic while I tried to figure out something to say, I rubbed at my eyes with my palms. "I wouldn't ask you to do that for me. Your thing is more important."

"How is my thing more important than yours? You want to join the equestrian team; if I took your assignment, you could."

"Yeah, and you'd be stuck in the bowels of the school doing people's dirty laundry and you would be giving up seeing Dave all the time. Not to mention your assignment sounds like fun and not dark ages drudgery."

She finally looked at me. "So you're not mad at me?"

"You think I didn't ask you because I was mad at you for something?"

She shrugged. "Helping is what I do."

I glanced up at all the posters on her walls. "Yeah, I get that."

"I'll do it," she declared.

Now I was sure she was drunk. "Emmie, no."

She nodded. "Yes. I want to."

"You're nuts."

"Maybe."

"Emmie, tonight was the hardest most physical two hours of my entire life. I can't ask you to take it. You'll end up hating me."

"Never," she said, with a decisive head shake. "I want to do it. Brooklyn, really. Let me do this for you."

I couldn't imagine any reason why she would do this, unless. "Is something wrong between you and Dave?"

"No," she said immediately. "Dave has nothing to do with it. This is between you and I. Dave is great, and spending more time with him would be awesome, but I try to live outside my comfort zone to remind me that other people don't have everything they want. I was being all elitist earlier when I said I was happy about the assignment and if it was due to nepotism, well, I definitely don't want it. I'd rather see you do it and get to be on the equestrian team."

"And anyway," she continued, flexing her biceps. "I could use to work out in the mornings."

I took a deep breath and considered what she'd said. It made me feel terribly elitist, but even more than that, lucky to have her as a friend and roommate. "Jeez, you make it seem like I'll be doing you a favor. How can I refuse?"

She threw her arms around me in what I was starting to know as an Emmie hug.

"So what do I have to do, just report in tomorrow morning?" she asked when we parted.

"We've got to take a signed affidavit or something to the dean's office, so I'd better go tomorrow morning. That means you have tonight to reconsider."

She shook her head. "Not a chance. I want to do this."

"Have you ever done laundry? Your own or anyone else's?" I asked.

She laughed. "Yes, freshman year. Why do you think my parents donated a building?" She clicked off my lamp.

"Back to sleep for you. Sweet dreams, roomie," she said, getting up off my bed as I lay back down. "I promise to be quiet," she whispered.

But I was already ninety percent asleep.

The next morning, after my crack-of-dawn stint down at the laundry and a hurried breakfast, Emmie and I went to the dean's office with the letter she'd drafted for us. I'd thought the secretary would have just taken it for us, to be delivered to the dean later, but no, the dean herself was available to discuss it with us.

Perfect.

We sat in the outer office chairs, waiting as I had before, but not for long, thankfully. Emmie and I chatted about our schoolwork; a boring topic suitable for the secretary's ears, only getting a few minutes in when the dean's door opened and she called for us. Emmie, looking a thousand times more at ease than I was, jumped up out of her chair and I followed her into the dragon's den.

I closed the door behind me and stepped toward the chairs, astonished when Emmie plunked herself down in one of them, even before the dean got her rump down in her own.

Undecided on how to proceed, I stood until the dean waved me toward the empty chair. "Sit."

I did, feeling more comfortable than if I was standing, but my back was still rod straight, like I was afraid she'd call me on bad posture.

"So, ladies. I understand you're here to swap your community service assignments."

Emmie handed her the letter she'd drawn up. "Yes, ma'am. Brooklyn will do the student liaison and I will do laundry."

The dean looked at Emmie for a moment, her face contorted in an expression of extreme concentration, like she wasn't sure what to say.

But Emmie spoke next, sparing her. "And I'd appreciate it if you wouldn't mention this to my parents. Although I'm sure you'd appreciate another significant endowment, I don't need to deal with their elitist hissy fit over their daughter doing laundry."

The dean pursed her lips before saying, "Ms. Prescott didn't coerce you into this, did she?"

"Nope," Emmie said casually. "Actually, I offered."

The dean gave her a curt nod. "And how are the plans coming for the dance next week? You've been working with your Westwood counterpart, as I understand it."

Emmie smiled. "The plans are going very well, thank you."

"Fine. You will see that project through to completion at the dance next Friday, and then the following week, you may switch. Until that time," the dean paused, looking at me. "You will continue your assignment in the laundry, Ms. Prescott."

I can't say I wasn't slightly disappointed about having to do more laundry, but it seemed fair, especially when Emmie was going to be doing it for the rest of the year. Another week and a day of laundry probably wouldn't kill me.

The First Practice

By Sunday morning, I was starting to get used to waking up at stupid o'clock, so I was at the stables well before seven, even having stopped at the dining hall to grab an apple and yogurt to eat on the way. Truth be told, I wasn't exactly hungry. I was nervous to be joining today's practice. Really nervous.

Not only was the pressure on to perform, since Brady had exempted me from tryouts, sight unseen, but I was seeing him for the first time since that night I'd signed up. And today, I wouldn't be seeing him as Brady, the friendly stable boy; I'd be seeing him as Coach Fleming, instructor and Olympian.

My five blue ribbons felt really lame and insignificant next to what must have been a whole case full of trophies and ribbons. Maybe two trophy cases. And then I thought of what Emmie had said about him being delicious, which made me even more nervous. Because he was, and that he was an Olympian made him just a tiny bit more attractive.

I made my way over to the stables, hearing voices as I approached, wishing I'd come earlier. I'd always enjoyed helping getting the horses ready; it always seemed to secure the bond between horse and rider. Or at least feel each other's mood out before getting into the arena. Being in sync was so important in riding, especially dressage.

The big doors were open, exposing the center aisle of the stable on both ends.

That's when I first saw Coach Fleming. He stood, helping another student saddle Poppy who was secured in the crossties. And as though he heard me taking him in from his long boots to his tight breeches, navy polo shirt and up to his ruffled black hair, he lifted his head and those amber eyes focused on me.

I had to force myself to breathe and continue toward him, my heart pounding hard in my chest.

He said something to the girl that I couldn't hear and then broke away from her to approach me. "Good morning, Ms. Prescott."

My last name sounded weird coming from his lips.

I nodded. "Coach Fleming."

His eyes wrinkled at the corners as he worked at hiding a mischievous smile.

"I'm not amused," I said, sounding to my own ears like someone's disappointed grandmother. When had I gotten so stodgy? Oh yeah, when he made a fool out of me. "You could have told me who you were," I hissed.

He turned his head and looked over his shoulder. The girl had stopped tacking Poppy to watch us. "Later," he said softly and then continued in a louder voice. "You'll be riding Charlie today. He's second from the end on the left. Why don't you head down and get to know each other. I'll be down in a few minutes."

I took a breath and nodded, walking past him, my arms crossed. "You should have told me," I breathed, just loud enough for him to hear me.

"Oh and Ms. Prescott?"

Stopping in my tracks, I turned back toward him.

All traces of humor were gone from his eyes. "I haven't had the opportunity to tell you before today, but you're to be here a half hour before practice to tack your horse. Keep that in mind for future."

I narrowed my eyes at him. "I will. Anything else, *sir*?"

"Yes. You're welcome."

You're welcome? Ugh. And he looked so smug when he said it. But the truth was, I did have him to thank for being on the team and, indirectly, for the reassignment that was going to get me out of doing laundry in Sub-basement B. Only five more days in that hellhole. Thank God, although I did feel a pang of guilt for Emmie. Though, she did offer.

But I didn't have the time to think about that now; I had a horse to saddle.

Saying nothing more, I turned back toward the barn and walked away.

~♥~

It turned out I had every reason to be nervous about my first day on the equestrian team.

There were five of us, which was a lot less than were signed up on the form in the stables. That was my first clue that I was going to be among really skilled riders; the cream of the crop hand-picked by the coach. These girls had probably been on horses their whole lives and even took private lessons in the summers.

I, on the other hand, hadn't been on a horse in over two years. To say I was rusty was an understatement. And now I was on a team with an Olympian for an instructor who only put me on the team because he assumed I was good.

I was not good. In fact, I was terrible. And everyone in the arena knew it.

Especially the coach. I could feel his disappointment every time he called out a direction across the arena. And I now understood why Emmie called him broody; he didn't smile once the entire time, he was all business as he took us through warm-ups and basic drills for this, our first official practice.

Thanks to it being the first one and him going easy on us (a fact I wouldn't have known if it weren't for Coach Fleming helpfully informing us) I managed to get through the practice without falling off or dying, but I knew there would be much suffering later from almost five hours of riding. What was worse than the impending physical pain was the humiliation over being nowhere near the caliber of the other riders.

Despite my exhaustion and the tightening of my muscles, I was brushing Charlie in the barn when the steady scrape of boots against the concrete told me the coach was approaching.

Awesome.

All the other girls were gone, but I was lingering behind and moving slowly as I finished up with Charlie and the tack. Mostly because I wasn't sure if my wobbly legs would take me all the way back to the dorm.

I felt him beside me and didn't turn away from the horse, making wide circles with the currycomb.

I took a breath but couldn't face him, knowing what was coming. "I'm sorry," I said.

"For what?" He actually sounded like he had no idea what I might be apologizing for. I turned to look at him.

And almost bumped into his chest, he was so close. I backed up, landing against Charlie's flank. Brady's hand reached out to steady my arm, his grip gentle but firm through my sweater.

I swallowed. "For making you think I was better than I am."

He let go of my arm and scrubbed his face with his hands. "I went out on a limb for you."

I looked down at my hands, and rubbed the base of my right thumb, working at the ache that was settling in after the hard practice. "I know you did. I was bragging about those stupid ribbons. I don't know why. I should have been at the tryouts and you would have seen that I wasn't any good."

"You're right; I should have made you try out. But that's on me."

"So I guess I'm off the team."

"I didn't say that."

I laughed. "No, but you were going to. I'll save you the trouble. I quit. I had no business being in that arena today."

"That's not true."

With a snort, I looked up at him. "You would have put me on the team if I'd tried out?"

He hesitated.

"That's what I thought," I said, returning to brushing Charlie. "Well you're off the hook—like I said, I'm quitting and you won't have to see me again until our equestrian unit in P.E."

"I never said you were off the team," he said, an edge to his voice, making me turn back toward him.

"Why?"

"You're not horrible, Brooklyn...Ms. Prescott," he corrected.

"Yes I am."

The corner of his mouth twisted up just a tiny bit. "Okay, you're slightly horrible. But here's the thing. I told the dean you were awesome and if you're suddenly off the team, I'm screwed."

I'd never thought about that; how he'd put himself on the line because of my stupid bragging.

"So now what?"

"You stay on the team."

I exhaled. "I don't know."

He cocked his head. "Come on, training for dressage, even if you're not going to make the Olympic team, has to be better than doing laundry, isn't it?"

He had a point. But... "That's another thing," I said, crossing my arms, dangling the currycomb in my fingers. "Why didn't you tell me you were the coach? I thought you were just a stable boy. You made me feel like an idiot."

He ran his fingers through his hair, making his biceps bulge under his polo shirt. "I apologize for that. It wasn't my intention; I didn't set out to deceive you."

"So why?" His eyes were on me and he was still standing close, too close, maybe, but I had nowhere to go since I was already backed up against a horse.

He looked away, down the aisle of the barn before he blew out a breath and said, "All the other girls know me. They know I'm the coach and am going to the Olympics. They don't see me: *Brady*. You looked at me differently."

I thought back to that first night, trying to remember how I'd looked at him, what I'd seen. Just a regular guy, I guess. Would I have seen him differently if I'd known he was the coach?

Definitely.

"Still," I said. "You should have told me before I left here that second time. That could have been really embarrassing."

"What's embarrassing is that you flirted with me to keep me from finding out about your friend making out with her boyfriend out back."

I did a double-take. "You knew about that?"

He gave me a guilty grin. "I saw them outside when I came in."

I gave his shoulder a push. "You knew the whole time?"

"Yeah. But I didn't know you were in on it until you were so desperate to get me away from the office, you used your feminine wiles."

My face heated up. "Um, as I remember it, you flirted with me first," I said cursing that my brain had let the word 'first' fall out of my mouth. But it was too late now. "You were the one talking about billiard balls in my pockets."

Now *he* was blushing. Which about made me melt into a pile of teenage hormones right there.

"I suppose I'm guilty of that. But you can't blame me. I thought you were here to see me, but I guess it was Charlie who had turned your head."

My mouth went instantly dry as I looked at him, his eyes unwavering on mine. My heart thudded in my chest and all I could think was *delicious, delicious, delicious.*

"I should finish up with Charlie," I croaked after an awkwardly long moment stretched between us.

He pursed his lips. "We still have a problem."

What now?

"If you're going to stay on the team, you need to get better. Fast."

"I didn't say I was going to stay on the team."

His eyes flared. "I put my ass on the line for you. You're staying on the team."

Defiant, I crossed my arms. "And if I don't?"

He shrugged, exasperated. "I can't stop you from quitting, but I don't just want you to stay so my ass is spared."

"Why then?" I asked, pushing away the guilt.

"Because I think you have potential," he said, and then looked away.

I tapped my foot, bringing his attention back to me. "And?"

He paused, but then looked into my eyes again, his like liquid honey. "Because I want you to."

My breath caught, but I faked a cough to cover it up. "Fine. I'll stay on the team. And I'll work hard to get better, but I won't even be at practice this week; I have to do the laundry assignment. I don't suppose you can get me out of that."

He exhaled and shook his head. "Not a chance. Can you be here in the evenings?"

I nodded before I even thought about what that would mean.

"Good. Be here right after dinner. I'll have Charlie saddled and ready to go. We'll get you there. Like I said, you have potential; you just need to work it."

"Thank you," I said, genuinely grateful for his faith in me and willingness to work with me to help me improve.

He nodded and gave Charlie a friendly stroke, slowly running his hand down the horse's shoulder. I watched the graceful movement of his arm, mesmerized.

He finished with a final pat. "Make sure you take a hot bath tonight."

For some reason, that made me blush again. "I will," I said, returning to Charlie as he left.

But I couldn't help myself; I turned my head to watch Brady walk away. And as I did, my heart lurched when I realized he'd also turned, to look at me.

Preparations

The five days that followed Sunday's dressage practice passed in a blur of exhaustion such as I'd never known before. I was in a constant state of physical agony as I continually punished my body: in the morning at the laundry, hefting sheets and towels in bundles that outweighed me, and then in the evening at the private practices in the arena with Brady. The only respite was during classes, where I fought to stay awake and keep out of trouble. Thankfully, English and French were a breeze, so I only really had to worry about science and then not literally falling over in P.E.

By the time I got to Friday, all I wanted to do was fall into bed and sleep for a week, but that wasn't on Emmie's agenda.

"You're going to the dance," she declared that afternoon in our room after last period.

My laying face down on my bed should have been her tip off that I had other plans for the evening. "No," I muttered into my pillow. "I'm dead. Leave me to decompose in peace."

She was having no part of it. "You have twenty minutes to nap, then we're going to dinner. Then back here to get ready."

"No dinner," I moaned, too tired to care about food.

She exhaled. "Fine. But when I get back, you're getting ready for the dance. You don't want to miss your opportunity to see your guy, do you?"

I didn't. Not that Will was *my guy*, but still...

"Come on, Brooklyn, Brady's going to be waiting for you. You can't disappoint him by being a no-show."

Brady, not Will. I wasn't surprised that Emmie would mention my coach. I'd downplayed the Will thing, since the further I got from that first day, the more I realized it had probably been nothing. If he'd been flirting at all, it was just to be friendly. And even if it had been real interest, I kept telling myself that a few minutes of joking around wasn't the real thing. I was not a believer in instalove. So said the rational part of my brain. Although when I closed my eyes, I could still see that smirk and his ocean-blue eyes looking back at me.

Get over it, Brooklyn, I told myself. At least three times a day.

The Brady thing, though, well, that had gotten a bit weird. When we were in the arena, he was all business: Coach Fleming. But back in the barn? He was all Brady; flirty Brady who was starting to make my insides tremble when he got close and his voice dropped to that low murmur he used when it was just us.

Emmie knew I had been with him every night and figured something was going on besides the hard-core training. I'd assured her nothing had happened, but she'd waved me off and said it was just a matter of time. She was probably right, though it felt weird and sordid—although he was still a high school student, he was technically off limits. All my new friends thought I was nuts. Maybe I was.

But it was a moot point, for tonight, anyway. Brady had told me he wasn't going to the dance. I didn't ask why, but I had a feeling he needed to catch up on some of his own training, since he'd been working with me so much. I felt a bit guilty about that, but he kept promising me he wasn't falling behind, so I tried to take him at his word.

"Brooklyn!" Emmie barked.

Rolling to my side and pulling my comforter over me, I said, "I'll get up, I promise. I just really need a little rest first."

"I'll be back in one hour," Emmie said just before I heard the door close softly behind her.

What felt like no more than one minute later (but was probably closer to the hour, as promised), she was back, waking me up from the sleep of the dead.

"Brooklyn!" she said, plunking down on my bed. "Get up. It's time to get ready."

I exhaled and forced myself to get out of bed and stumble toward the bathroom for a shower. Five minutes later, I was leaning against the tile, eyes closed and enjoying the soothing hot water in a near trance, when the spray turned ice cold. I screamed and opened my eyes to see my roommate standing beside the shower stall, a determined look on her face and a hand on the hot tap.

"Let's go!" she said.

It appeared my roommate, the save-the-world poster child for altruism, had a take no prisoners attitude when it came to getting her roommate ready for a dance.

I both loved and hated her for it.

"I'm coming. I'll be out in a few."

"No sleeping in the shower."

I shivered, turning the cold water off. "Yeah, not much chance of that happening now. I need to dry my hair and do my face."

She was finishing her makeup, leaning close to the mirror to do her mascara, her mouth agape as she concentrated on covering each lash. "It'll be dark in the gym, so make sure you wear a bit more makeup than usual to be dramatic."

"How long do I have?"

She glanced down at the phone on the counter. "Bus leaves for Westwood in a half-hour."

I cursed. That was barely enough time. I hadn't even picked out anything to wear yet—not that I had a lot of outfits to choose from. We wore uniforms to classes and then most of the rest of my wardrobe was jeans and pajamas. I had exactly two dresses that my mother had sent me with, just in case. We hadn't really thought about dances; who figures they need anything nice to wear at an all-girls school?

"What are you wearing?" I asked, reaching for the towel and wrapping it around me.

"The Fendi," she said, as though I could identify parts of her wardrobe by designer.

"Oh, God, that was pretentious," she said, shaking her head. "I'm sorry. The black dress. The one with the lace on top."

"Hello?" Chelly called out from the door.

"We're in here," Emmie called back.

Chelly materialized in the bathroom doorway wearing a tight and curvy dress in fire-engine red, which should have looked gaudy with her red hair, but didn't. She looked like a bombshell.

"Wow," I said, giving her the once over.

"Right?" she said, her wide smile confident. I wished I had a quarter of her self-assurance. Hell, I bet any girl did—if you could bottle that stuff and sell it, you'd be an instant millionaire.

Emmie turned away from the mirror and took in Chelly. "You look Ah-ma-zing!"

"Thanks, girls. Brooklyn! You're in a towel! Are you going to be ready in time?"

"Yeah, sure," I said. "As soon as I figure out what I'm going to wear." It was a joke, since I had such a narrow choice.

Emmie and Chelly exchanged a shocked look. "You don't know what you're wearing yet?" Chelly asked, scandalized. I suppose if I hadn't been slaving in the laundry and working my ass off in the equestrian arena, maybe I would have put some more thought or care into tonight, but as it was, I was barely awake.

"You should borrow my Stella McCartney," Emmie announced. "You've got the body for it."

"No, it's okay. I don't need to borrow your clothes," I was starting to feel anxious as it was; I didn't need to worry about her *très* expensive wardrobe, too.

Chelly disappeared and returned holding up a black dress with a black and white heart print on top. "This one?"

Emmie nodded. "Yeah, it will look amazing on you, Brooklyn. Just try it on. But hurry up, we have eighteen minutes!"

On the Way to the Dance

The bus ride to Westwood was surreal. After two weeks of stewing in estrogen, save a few male teachers, the Rosewood girls were crazy excited to be going to the dance where they would experience, as Chelly put it, the Westwood Buffet. The buzz on the bus was palpable and I could only describe it as something like a shark feeding frenzy, where the sharks wore designer dresses and a lot of makeup and were very, very hungry.

I'd only met a few of the guys: Will, Evan and I guess Brady counted, too, since he was a student, along with Dave, who I hadn't yet met, but had heard enough about to know was pretty much perfection on a stick, but to hear the girls talk, all Westwood boys were great catches.

Money, looks, smarts—just like Rosewood girls had it all, Westwood boys did, too. Plus testosterone and muscles—Westwood prided itself on having an excellent athletics program and boasted the highest number of Olympic podium finishes per capita of any school in the U.S.

"Why so quiet?" Chelly asked from the seat in front of me. She was sitting sideways so she could talk to all of us as we sat together on the short ride to the Westwood campus.

I shrugged, "Tired I guess." And I was, but that wasn't why I was quiet. I was terrified.

Sure, I had been to dances before and even some big non-school ones back in London. I had some okay moves on the floor, but that's not what I was worried about: this was different. This was my first dance as the *new and improved* Brooklyn, who was going to try to embrace the fact that she was the new girl and get herself noticed.

I had to admit, if ever I was prepped to be noticed, this was it. The designer dress, which Emmie had practically forced onto my body, did look exceptional on me. And my makeup somehow came together with only one rushed mascara wand to the eyeball. My strappy pumps, though being higher than what I was used to, completed the outfit and made my legs look great, despite them causing new discomfort in my already aching calves. But I'd power through. This was the dance, the one that was going to set the tone for the entire year.

"I can't wait to see Dave," Emmie said, bouncing in her seat a little beside Chelly, making her move up and down, too.

"You just saw him last night when you set up the gym for the dance," I said, remembering how she'd returned the night before with googly eyes and plumped lips that I knew were from making out and not some cosmetic lip enhancer.

She gave me a sheepish look, as though she was remembering, too. "Well yeah, but they'll be wearing jackets and ties tonight. They all look so sexy when they're dressed up."

"Bring it!" Chelly said. "I can't wait."

We all laughed, which eased my nerves a bit. Though I realized I wasn't the only quiet one. "So, is there anyone you have your eye on?" I asked Kaylee. She was sitting beside me in a subdued, but very pretty navy dress accented by a small diamond pendant. Although I didn't know many of the boys, she'd had two years to get to know them and single out at least one.

She shook her head and opened her mouth to say something, but Celia interrupted before she got the chance.

"She had a thing for Phillip Carson last year, but then he started dating Harmony Wilson. They're both seniors this year."

"They're not still together," Chelly broke in. "They broke up during the summer."

Kaylee's eyes lit up as she looked at Chelly. "Really?"

Chelly nodded. "Yep. Harmony hooked up with a guy back home. She's doing the long distance thing—I heard her talking about it in Algebra."

"Will you dance with him?" I asked.

Kaylee shrugged. "I don't think so."

94

"Yes she will," Celia said. "We'll make it happen. Kaylee, don't think about..."

Kaylee cut her off with a look. I wondered what that was about, but Celia shook her head when I looked at her.

"He's friends with Dave," Emmie said. "I'll talk to him."

"How are you going to talk and make out at the same time?" Chelly asked, her face deadpan.

Emmie playfully smacked her, but didn't bother answering, turning to me. "I can't wait for you to meet Dave," she said. "You're going to love him. Well, not love him, love him, but you'll get along great when you do the liaison thing together."

I'd forgotten that when Emmie traded Community Service Assignments with me that it meant I would get to work with her boyfriend.

"Brooklyn's met Dave," Chelly said, looking from Emmie to me.

"Not yet," I said.

Chelly frowned and looked at Celia. "I'm sure he was who helped you move your trunk upstairs when they screwed up your room. Him and Jenks. Right, Celia?"

Celia nodded and looked at me. "Yeah, when they brought your trunk to my room."

I glanced at Emmie. "No," I said, starting to panic. "He said his name was Will."

"Willmont Davidson," Emmie said. "He goes by Dave. Just like Evan goes by Jenks. That's what they all do."

I looked at my roommate and tried to force my heart out of my throat. "Emmie, I swear..."

She looked at me weirdly for a half a second and then waved me off, her mouth breaking into a smile. "It's okay. But did he really tell you his name was Will? He hates his first name."

I thought back to that first day. "No," I shook my head. "It was a misunderstanding. He said his name was Willmont and I guess I shortened it to Will. He didn't correct me. Emmie, I..."

She shook her head. "No, seriously. It's okay. He's a total flirt. I get it. I guess I should be flattered that you think he's hot, right?" she laughed, but it was a bit strained. Like she was trying to be the big person.

But it was suddenly awkward. The guy she'd been talking about for two weeks; the perfect, sexy and smart guy who was an amazing kisser turned out to be the same guy I'd been secretly pining over.

And was going to be spending the year working with.

"Dave is a flirt," Kaylee said. "But he's not the cheating type. And anyway, we all know he's absolutely in love with you, Emmie."

"And anyway, you've got Brady, right?" Celia said, also trying to ease the tension.

We all looked at her and I could have hugged her and Kaylee in that moment.

"Right," I said. "Brady."

"He's totally into you," Chelly said. "I saw you talking to him the other day outside the stables. He's never shown any interest in anyone before, but he was looking at you like he wanted to throw you down on the floor of the stables. It was hot." She made a point of fanning herself with her hand.

I glanced at Emmie, who seemed to be relieved at that.

"He's totally sexy," Celia said. "Those eyes. Rowr."

We all laughed. Things were almost back to normal.

Almost.

But on the inside I was still panicking that later Emmie was going to remember what I'd said about liking the trunk mover guy and she was going to hate me.

My heart began to pound as we pulled up to the Westwood driveway. My objective for the evening had just done a one-eighty. I was no longer eager to see Willmont Davidson again; I was desperate to avoid him at all costs.

The Westwood Restroom

The good thing about being in panic mode? Adrenaline floods your body and your extreme exhaustion gives way to a kind of hysterical mania. The good news: I no longer felt like I was dying of fatigue. The bad news: my fight or flight response had been engaged and I wanted nothing more than to run the five miles or so back to Rosewood. In heels.

But with my friends gathered close, that wasn't going to happen, so the best I could hope for was damage control.

The bus pulled up to the front doors of Westwood, but before we could get off, the dean boarded and gave us a big lecture about being on our best behavior. We were warned not to go into boys' rooms or darkened hallways and that any lewd or inappropriate behavior (Chelly made a gesture, shoving her left thumb into the cup of her right hand, making us all giggle) would get us removed from the dance and returned to Rosewood immediately. She also threatened us with a call home if that happened, which did cause a few straightened backs among my fellow students.

It was a moot point for me, so I wasn't worried.

As we all poured off the bus, most of the girls eager to get into Westwood as quickly as possible despite the dean's prohibitive warnings, I hung back with Kaylee, moving slowly to allow all the rest of the girls to get into the gym first. I figured my best plan of attack was to hang out in the bathroom for a few minutes and let everyone get situated before I made my entrance. Best to approach a scene like this with caution.

"You okay?" Kaylee asked quietly.

I looked over and gave her a half smile. "Yeah. It's just…weird, I guess."

She held the front door of the Westwood main building open for me, nodding me through. "You really had no idea?"

"None. I never would have gone on about him…" I rubbed my right temple as we walked, noting that Westwood looked a lot like Rosewood: lots of marble and rich wood, though it smelled different, more masculine. Even just an hour before, I would have been drawn to it, but now, it was like the smell of impending disaster.

"God, Kaylee, I feel like such an idiot."

"If you didn't know, it's not your fault." She lowered her voice. "He is just about the hottest guy here, so there's no faulting your taste."

I gave her a look. "You, too?"

She shrugged. "I'm not after him or anything, but come on, he's the whole package, right?"

I wasn't about to argue. And I'd known a guy like that had to be taken already; foolish to think for a second that he might have been interested in me. I looked around. "Where's the bathroom?"

"This way." Kaylee's hand landed on my shoulder as she guided me away from the crowd we were following and down a quiet hallway. "Don't worry about it. It'll blow over. Emmie's not the jealous type, and it's not like anything happened with him. Right?" She looked at me pointedly, like she was waiting for me to agree with her.

"Of course not! He just helped me with my stuff. He was really nice, just like I said. That's all. I guess…I don't know. Maybe at the time I thought there was more to it. I don't have a lot of experience with boys, obviously."

Kaylee nodded and pushed through the door into the ladies' restroom. "You're not alone. I'm not too popular at these things, either."

Kaylee was shy and quiet—definitely a bookworm, but she was pretty and really funny once you got to know her. I hooked my arm through hers. "It's you and me, girlfriend. Let's make a pact: we will both slow dance with at least one hot guy tonight."

She looked at me like she was going to be ill. "I don't know, Brooklyn. It's a miracle I'm even here. I don't think I'm up for anything like that."

I frowned. "What does that mean? Is this about what Celia was talking about on the bus?

She looked under the stall doors, and when she made sure we were alone, she leaned against the sink counter and crossed her arms. "You didn't hear about what happened last year." It wasn't a question. I shook my head anyway. "What happened?"

Avoiding my eyes, she fidgeted her hands.

"Kaylee?"

She looked up at me. "It's so humiliating."

I couldn't even imagine what had happened to Kaylee, but whatever it was, it was making her blush and fidget just by thinking about it. I wasn't about to push her, but I could tell she wanted to tell me.

She swallowed. "I barfed."

"What?"

"At last year's holiday dance, right before Christmas. I had the flu but didn't know it. I was dancing with the girls during a fast song and Phillip was there with us. I think maybe he had been interested, too. Next thing I knew, I got super hot; I thought it was from the dancing, but no."

"Oh God," I said sympathetically.

"Yeah. The worst part is I did it right there on the dance floor. Some of it even hit Phillip's pants. I almost died."

"Oh, Kaylee, I'm so sorry."

She shrugged. "I haven't been to a dance since. The girls say everyone's over it, but I don't know. I..." she exhaled loudly.

I gave her a hug then pulled away, still holding her shoulders. "Okay, look. We're obviously a couple of social misfits who are going to be kind of under the microscope at this dance tonight. We'll stick together, but I still think we should do that pact thing. We both need to cleanse our palates with some cute guys."

She looked unsure. "I don't know, Brooklyn."

"I do," I said, exuding a confidence that I didn't really feel but figured I could fake my way through. "Come on. We'll get through this together."

    She took a deep breath and nodded. "Okay. Let's do it."

The Gym Arrival

Kaylee and I walked into the gym together, though I'm not sure which one of us was more nervous. I gave her a smile, which she returned.

Sort of. Okay, maybe *she* was more nervous.

I looked around to try to find our friends, which wasn't easy among the loud music and dim lights punctuated by moving spots and strobes.

"Over there," Kaylee said, pointing to the right side of the room that had been decorated with streamers and posters of our schools' crests. Not the most fun decorations, but the music was good, and as we walked over to our friends, I saw most people were smiling and laughing, so that was what really mattered.

And it didn't appear Will...*Dave* was with Emmie, so that was a plus. I scanned around just to make sure, but the look on her face as she bit her lip anxiously and did a room scan of her own, told me he wasn't there. I felt bad for her, but relieved nonetheless

Her face brightened as we approached. "There you two are! We were getting worried you'd gone back to Rosewood."

"Nope," I said. *Even though the thought* had *occurred to me*, I didn't say.

"Just a little bio break," Kaylee explained.

"So..." I began, hoping someone would fill us in on the lay of the land so far.

"Dave's not here yet," Emmie said. "That's the problem with the dance being at their campus; they wander down when they feel like it. He was supposed to be here by now." She clucked her tongue; I couldn't tell if she was angry or nervous. Maybe a bit of both.

I looked around and realized the Rosewood girls probably made up something like eighty percent of the bodies in the room.

"Don't worry," Celia said. "Once they realize we're here, they'll come down. They are boys, after all. Come on, let's get a soda," she grabbed my arm and led Kaylee and I over to the 'bar', set up with sodas and juices. There were also plenty of snacks, which my empty stomach appreciated, since I'd skipped supper.

And then, just as I reached for a bag of Doritos, I heard Chelly announce the boys had arrived, her voice an almost inaudible purr over the music.

"They're here."

As one, we turned and looked at the dozen or so boys that headed the pack. Perhaps we seemed predatory, but in fairness, our interest was matched by that of the new arrivals as they looked around, taking us in.

And, I had to admit, they deserved our attention, because they all looked good in their suits, complete with fancy pocket squares in various colors. They were clean, their hair brushed and styled, and I imagined they probably took as much care in getting ready for this dance as we had. Actually, in my case, probably more.

We were all on display for each other.

"This is like a weird social experiment," I said to Kaylee.

She nodded, keeping her gaze on her soda.

"What does Phillip look like?" I asked.

Her head snapped up. "What?"

"You're going to dance with him, right?"

She gave me a terrified look. "Oh I don't think so. I can't dance with *him*."

"Yes you can. It was a long time ago. And it's just a dance. What does he look like?"

She took a sip of her soda and discreetly looked around. "There. On the right in that group with four other guys. He's the second tallest one with the dark hair and glasses."

I followed her gaze to the group of boys and pinpointed him easily. He was obviously the leader of his group, talking and laughing exuberantly while the boys around him seemed to hang on his every word. It was immediately obvious why Kaylee was into him: she saw him as everything she wasn't. Charismatic, confident, popular. I knew the type.

She was going to have her work cut out for her, getting close to him.

And then, out of the corner of my eye, I saw Emmie rush to the doorway. That could only mean one thing: Dave.

I made a point of turning my back on them, which was stupid, but I didn't want her to think I was watching for him.

"Oh God," Kaylee said.

My heart started thudding in my chest, but I forced myself not to turn. "What?"

"I think she's getting Dave to go talk to Phillip."

Whew. "That's *good*, Kaylee."

"I don't know. He's so good looking and popular...Oh my God, he's looking over here. They both are. Brooklyn, what do I do?"

It was tempting to laugh, but more out of my own nervousness than thinking she was being ridiculous. "Stay cool. Keep talking to me. Conjugate some French verbs for me."

She looked into my eyes and swallowed, but she understood.

"*Je suis, tu es...*"

"Good," I said, nodding. Hoping she'd lose the wild-eyed look. "Keep going."

"*Nous sommes, vous êtes.* Oh my God, Brooklyn. They're coming over here. *Ils sont* ....."

"You can stop doing French. Just be cool."

"Right. Uh, so, where did you get your dress?"

"Emmie's closet. Do you like it?"

She never got the chance to answer because at that second, our cozy group of two became a bloated and awkward group of eight.

"Hi girls," Emmie said sort of woodenly.

"Phillip, this is Brooklyn and you remember Kaylee."

I imagined Phillip *couldn't help* but remember the girl who vomited on him, but he smiled politely at both of us.

"Nice to meet you," he said to me and gave Kaylee a nod. A good sign.

"And Dave," Emmie said, "This is my roommate Brooklyn, but I think you've met. Though she thought your name was Will." She laughed, but the humor in her voice was like velvet over steel. She wasn't over it and I needed to tread lightly or it was going to be the worst year ever, stuck with a roommate who hated me.

"Hi," I said to him, looking somewhere over his shoulder. "Sorry, I thought..."

He waved me off. "It's okay. It technically is my name. I understand we're going to be working together on the student liaison."

Right. Suddenly the laundry was starting to look like the good option.

"Yes," I said, my brain pretty much stalling out.

"Wait," he said, his brow furrowing. "*You're* Emmeline's roommate?"

I nodded, looking at Emmie, but she just shrugged. Was this some sort of problem?

He glanced over at one of the boys standing just outside the group and gave him some sort of pointed look. The boy, who seemed older with his perma-stubble look and long hair pulled back into a ponytail gave him a microscopic nod, but I still caught it.

Like I wasn't already vibrating with nerves? What did *this* mean?

"What's going on?" Emmie demanded.

Will...*Dave*...looked down at her and gave one of his smirky smiles. "Nothing, Em. We thought someone else was your roommate this year, that's all." And whatever it was, was suddenly forgotten as she rolled her eyes and then smiled back. I fought a sigh, secretly wishing I'd been on the receiving end of that smile.

Emmie changed gears. "You and Brooklyn will get to coordinate the Halloween dance and, more importantly, the Thanksgiving food drive together," she said and I could hear her disappointment.

It was suddenly too much.

Despite the audience, I turned to her. "You know what? That is so much more your thing. I'm going to go back to the dean and change our assignments back."

She went wide-eyed. "No. I made this commitment, I want you to do it."

It made no sense. Why would she want to deny herself what was basically her dream assignment with *her boyfriend*?

"Emmie," I said, but she cut me off.

"No, Brooklyn, this is not negotiable."

I leaned in close. "It's weird."

She shook her head. "It's not weird. Seriously, I promise."

She was kidding herself. I stole a quick look at Dave; he was watching us with a slight frown on his face. A glance at the other guys told me they were wrapped up in their own conversation, leaving poor Kaylee on the outside, basically standing by herself, sipping her soda.

"Excuse us," I said to Dave and pulled Emmie away toward Kaylee.

"Emmie," I whispered. "I can't do this. I don't want you to always think there's something going on."

She looked at me and her brow furrowed angrily. "I trust you, Brooklyn."

"You don't *know* me," I said.

She crossed her arms. "Well I thought I did. Are you trying to tell me something?"

I realized what I'd just implied. "No! That's not what I meant. Just...I don't know, Emmie, it's really weird and I feel like such an idiot." I smoothed my hands down my thighs and realized I was wearing her dress, which just made it feel even more awkward.

Her face softened. "Okay, so I get your point. I guess two

weeks isn't really a long time to know someone, but I do trust you. And even more, Brooklyn, I trust Dave. So although, yes, it feels kind of awkward right now, it's not a big deal. We'll laugh about this in a few weeks when you and him pull off the best food drive ever."

"But why? Why are you doing this for me?"

She shrugged. "It's what I do. I saw how much you wanted to join the equestrian team. And anyway, I'm looking forward to my evenings free; I've sourced a new fair trade clothing company and am thinking of helping them open an e-store."

I just stared at her. She blinked, "What?"

Kaylee laughed. "Let me guess, you didn't realize Emmie was an e-commerce mogul?"

"Not even a little."

Emmie rolled her eyes, looking modest. "You've been too busy to see what I've been up to. And anyway, like I said, I haven't done anything for them yet, I've just been doing my research while you've been at the stables."

"Is there anything you *can't* do?" I exhaled. "Thank you so much, Emmie."

"And speaking of you at the stables, once you get with your broody, sexy coach, you won't give Dave another thought."

I rolled my eyes, ignoring the fluttering in my stomach. "Are you absolutely one-hundred percent sure you're good with this?"

"Better than good," she said, wrapping me into one of her hugs. As she did, the first slow song of the night came on. "In fact, to show you just how good, I think you should dance with him."

I pulled back away from her. "No."

"No, really. I'm okay with it. Come on, he's a good dancer."

That was supposed to make it better? Panic rose like bile in my throat. "Emmie, no."

I looked at Kaylee and she gave me a wide-eyed look that probably closely mirrored my own. The one that said, *"What the...?"*

But Emmie wouldn't be denied. She grabbed my hand and pulled me back toward the guys. Then, as an afterthought, she turned back and grabbed Kaylee, pulling her along.

It appeared we were both going to get to dance with hot guys.

What is it they say—be careful what you wish for?

Dancing

Despite Kaylee's desperate whispered protests and my sudden hope that the floor was going to open up and swallow me whole, Emmie succeeded in dragging us over to the guys.

Emmie on a mission was not to be denied.

"You guys," she said to the boys in her authoritative tone. "We all need dance partners. Dave, you go with Brooklyn, and Phillip, you're with Kaylee. I'll dance with Declan. You two..." she pointed at the two guys who had not yet been assigned and then looked around. Chelly was doing just fine on her own on the other side of the gym, circled by a group of guys, but Celia was hovering by the bar, talking with Chelly's roommate Naomi.

"Over there," Emmie continued, moving her point toward the girls. "Celia and Naomi."

As I stood there, basically paralyzed, I watched Phillip step toward Kaylee. She looked nervous but hopeful, and I was suddenly so happy for her.

Until he said, "You're not going to puke on me again, are you?"

Kaylee's face collapsed into a mask of despair. Exactly what she was afraid of had just happened, only worse. I looked from her to Emmie hoping she was going to kick the guy in the crotch.

But before either of us had a chance to do anything, one of the boys stepped forward, shouldering Phillip out of the way. "I'll dance with you," he said, looking down at Kaylee with a smile that could melt an iceberg. His deep Irish brogue made it that much sexier. Way sexier.

"Declan to the rescue," Dave said with a chuckle. "Shall we?"

It wasn't until I watched Kaylee smile and take Declan's outstretched hand that I realized Dave was talking to me.

"Oh, uh yeah."

I gave Emmie one last questioning look, but she nodded and waved us out to the dance floor. Losing her dance partner, she stayed where she was, but as I turned away, I saw her start to give Phillip what I'm sure was a few choice words about his behavior. A kick to the balls would have been my preference. Jerk.

"She's something, isn't she?" Dave said, bringing my attention back to him.

Right. *Dave*. "Yeah. She's a force of nature."

We stopped together at an arbitrary spot on the floor and I held my breath as his hands came to rest on my hips. He was barely touching me and in a way I'd been touched by boys before, but here and now, with him, it felt so close and very intimate. My heart thumped so hard, I was sure he could hear it.

With my heels on I was able to comfortably lay my arms on his shoulders, but I was careful to keep my distance, knowing Emmie would be watching. And anyway, the further I could stay away from him, the better. It was bad enough I could smell his cologne, a warm masculine scent, the same one from that first day, but stronger, more concentrated. It almost made me feel dizzy and I wondered if there were pheromones or something in it to make him extra attractive. If so, it was totally working.

Not good.

"So," he began as we started to move to the music, making small circles in the little spot we'd carved out.

"Yeah," I said. Because I had to say *something* and 'yeah' was the best my brain could do. I looked over his shoulder and watched my friends dancing. Kaylee seemed to be having a good time with Declan, laughing as they turned with the music. He was tall and lean with strawberry blond hair atop his rugged features. And that charming accent...

Dave's fingers pressed into my hips lightly, bringing my attention back to him.

"So, Emmeline says I'm not supposed to flirt with you."

I almost swallowed my tongue. "What?" I croaked.

He grinned, that smirky smile that was going to be the death of me.

"She said my flirting is going to get me into trouble."

My neurons were firing, but not in a way that I cold harness them into helping with something to say. I probably looked like a fish out of water, gaping at him.

"What?" he said. The smirk was suddenly gone from his face.

"*Going* to get you into trouble?" I managed.

He bit his full bottom lip, drawing my attention there, reminding me that Emmie'd gone on and on about him being an amazing kisser. Reminding me that I'd heard them out behind the stables.

"What do you mean?" he said.

It was almost too much. But I couldn't stop dancing with him. A glance over his shoulder and I could see Emmie watching. Not like she was pissed, but definitely keeping an eye on us.

I couldn't look anywhere without it being awkward. I suddenly focused on his pocket square, noting that it was kind of an odd color—bright orange against his dark suit. I'd only seen colors like that on groomsmen before. Then my eyes drifted to his chin where the hint of stubble showed. God help me, but it was sexy.

"I can't believe she made me dance with you," I muttered, suddenly wishing I was anywhere else. Even the laundry, seven hours into an eight-hour shift. In the middle of summer. With no A/C.

"Am I that horrible?" Dave asked.

I looked up and he was smiling, but it didn't reach his eyes.

Nice going, Brooklyn, totally insult the guy. "Ugh, I'm sorry. That's not what I meant." I shook my head. "It's just...we had a misunderstanding. It's fixed now. Don't worry about it."

"What kind of misunderstanding?"

Thankful for the dim lighting that was hopefully covering up the hot blush creeping up my cheeks, I said in as breezy a tone as I could muster, "It's nothing."

He paused long enough for me to think he'd dropped it and I began to relax and just enjoy the dance, concentrating on the feel of his hands on my hips, his minty breath mingling with the smell of him, the music we swayed to...

But he wasn't done. "Wait, Brooklyn...Did you...is that why she..."

"Never mind," I interrupted, my voice climbing involuntarily toward screechy. "It's not important." I looked over his shoulder again, pasting what I hoped was a neutral and non-awkward smile on my face.

"Brooklyn," he said, his voice quieter. "Did you come here to meet me, thinking I was someone else? Did you not know about me and Em?"

*Oh God...*Tears pricked at my eyes and my throat closed up. I shook my head and avoided his eyes.

"I'm so sorry," he said. "I never meant..."

"Just stop," I said, my voice barely above a whisper. "Please."

"I'm sorry," he said again.

I swallowed and kept looking over his shoulder, determined not to cry.

His hands squeezed at my hips and I almost bolted right then. Only knowing that Emmie was watching kept me dancing with him.

"Brooklyn?" he asked suddenly in a weird voice.

I exhaled and looked at his face.

"Any reason why Fleming is trying to kill me with his eyes right now?"

Brady? Turning, I followed his gaze to the edge of the dance floor where Brady stood in a jacket and tie. He did indeed look like he was trying to kill Dave with his eyes.

Dave looked at me, one eyebrow raised. "You have something going on with him that's making him act like a very jealous, rutting boar?"

I only had time to swallow and try to come up with

111

something to say before Dave then announced that Brady was on his way over. One song had morphed into another and some couples were trickling off the dance floor. I had a moment to notice Kaylee still dancing with Declan. But my other friends weren't in my field of vision.

"Brooklyn?" Brady materialized at my side.

"Hi," I said, not capable of much more.

"Fleming," Dave said with a nod, his fingers squeezing at my hips again. Not letting go.

"Can I have a turn?" Brady asked, looking at me as though Dave wasn't even there.

I nodded, removing my hands from Dave's shoulders. "Thanks," I said to him, not quite looking him in the eye as I shifted to Brady.

I'd never been more thankful for anything in my entire life as I was for that sudden interruption. I almost even thanked Brady, but bit my tongue; the last thing I wanted to do was explain *that* awkward situation. To a guy.

He smelled good, too, but completely different than Dave. Brady's scent was more earthy, less cologne and more of soap and just...guy, though the familiar smells of saddle soap and leather were absent, making me realize I'd never been with him outside the stables.

His hands slid around my waist, higher up than where Dave had held me. I put my arms on his shoulders, but he was taller and I had to clasp my hands around his neck. The back of his hair tickled my fingers. He gently pulled me closer, his large palms spanning my lower back. My breath caught.

"I thought you weren't coming?" I asked.

He shrugged under my arms, reminding me of his powerful shoulders. "I changed my mind. You look really good, Brooklyn."

I couldn't help but smile. "Thanks. You clean up pretty nice, too, Coach Fleming."

He closed his eyes for half a second and exhaled, his dark eyebrows knitting together, like I'd hurt him.

"Brady," I said.

He opened his eyes and looked at me, his eyes burning into mine. But it was too much, too intense, and I had to look away. But when I looked over his shoulder out at the rest of the crowd, I saw Dave dancing with Emmie.

And he wasn't looking at her.

He was looking at me.

So Much for that Day Off

"**B**rooklyn?"

I swung my eyes back to Brady's face, embarrassed to be caught looking at someone else. "Sorry."

"I wanted to talk to you about practice."

"Okay," I said, biting my lip, waiting for him to tell me he was going to cut me from the team. I'd improved over the week and had shaken off some of the cobwebs from not riding for a couple of years, but was still nowhere near as good as the other girls. There wasn't much chance I would ever be.

I wondered what Dean Haywood would do if I got cut from the team; would I get sent back to the laundry? It almost sounded like an appealing option. Glancing over at the crowd of faculty standing together near the bar (watching over the punchbowl, Celia had pointed out) I saw the dean looking over the dance floor. It had to be a trick of the sweeping lights, but it seemed like she was looking right at me. I quickly returned my eyes to Brady, shaking my head. "Sorry," I said again.

"You seem distracted," he said, giving me one of his signature smirks.

It made my heart do a little flutter. "There's a lot going on here. Remember, it's my first dance at here. So much stimulation."

"Right. Stimulation," he said, pulling me a little closer. As he did, my arms edged up a bit over his shoulders, my bare skin sliding against his muscular neck. He was warm against me, making gooseflesh rise on my arms, making my breath catch.

His eyes were like pools of liquid amber, intense, deep.

"Brady, I..." I began, but couldn't finish my sentence. I didn't even know what to say. The whole experience was scrambling my brain.

"Tomorrow," he said.

"What?"

"We should practice tomorrow."

"Oh," I breathed. It wasn't what I'd expected him to say, but then again, I wasn't at all sure what he was thinking.

"You're coming along really well, but I think you're still behind. We should keep up with the daily practices."

I had been looking forward to a day off. My legs and butt were *definitely* looking forward to a day off, and quite frankly, the heels I was wearing were killing my already stretched and cramped calves.

My eyes filled with tears as I thought about losing my one chance at a rest. Not normally a crier, I was shocked, but figured the exhaustion was catching up with me. Fighting the tears, I took a deep breath and nodded.

"You okay?" he asked. He was so intuitive—something I was sure either came from being around horses so much or maybe was something he was born with that made him such an exceptional rider, though I hadn't yet had the pleasure of seeing him in action.

"Yes," I said. "I'm fine. I'm just a bit tired. It's been a long week and I was sort of looking forward to sleeping in tomorrow." Many Rosewoods had their CSAs to catch up on over the weekend, but since mine had been fulfilled in the laundry through the week, I'd been granted a day off to do as I pleased. And what I pleased was sleeping in and then spending some quality time in the aquatic center's whirlpool to ease my overworked body. Also, I had a mountain of homework to catch up on.

Brady smiled. "You can sleep in. I have my own training in the early morning. If you meet me at the stables by eleven, that will give us a solid couple of hours before we have to get out of the way for the afternoon leisure riders."

I exhaled. "Okay. But as long as you promise me you're not cutting your training short to help me. I do not want to be the reason Westwood's favorite Olympian only gets a silver medal."

He snorted. "I'm not the school's favorite Olympian." He

nodded toward the group of boys hanging around Chelly. "Jenkins is the star here."

Surprised that I'd actually met *two* future Olympians, I asked, "What's his sport? Not another equestrian?"

Brady shook his head. "No. Diving. If all goes well, we'll be at the games together, but nowhere near the same sport."

I thought about them traveling together—it would be nice to have a familiar face during what must be a crazy stressful time. "Are you friends?"

Brady looked away from me, but not at the group of boys. It was like he had to think about his answer before he said, "Not really. I mean, we respect each other as athletes, and he's top notch in his sport. But friends? No."

I nodded, feeling awkward for having asked. My eyes drifted down to his suit jacket pocket and noticed something. "Why don't you have a pocket square?"

"Pardon?"

I looked around the gym. "Most of the other guys have pocket squares. A lot in really bright colors. You don't have one."

He looked out at the crowd over my shoulder. "I don't know. I'm sure it's something stupid. Anyway," he said, seemingly eager to change the subject. "About the Olympics. I'll be lucky to get a silver."

"Suffering a bout of lagging confidence, Coach Fleming?" I teased.

But his face got serious. "No, not lagging confidence, just being realistic. I'm good...okay, some might say *great*," he paused, looking a little embarrassed, which I have to admit was way sexy. "But I'm not gold medal material. I know that, and it's okay," he quickly added when I opened my mouth to protest.

"Really, Brooklyn. Not everyone can win, but to move up my ranking or even get a bronze or silver? That would be a dream come true."

"But shouldn't you aim for the top?"

He shrugged, making my arms slide against his neck again,

a movement I tried to ignore, though futilely. I swallowed, cursing my suddenly dry throat.

"I'm aiming for a personal best. It'd be different if I competed in marathons or a team sport with an obvious opponent on the field with me. But you know as well as I do that equestrian is different; your partner doesn't care about medals or acclaim or the millions of people watching. If Albatross has a bad day, I'm screwed. But I will hope we have a great day and I make no errors. That we're in sync and the magic happens. That's what it's really about."

"Your horse's name is Albatross?" I asked.

He nodded, smiling. "I'll get to see him soon."

"Oh?"

"He'll be here in less than a week. Well, not here, exactly. The stables where I train are about twenty miles from here."

The smile on his face was so open, genuine, I could tell exactly how he felt about his horse and reuniting with him. "You've missed him," I said.

He nodded. "Very much. The other horses at the training center are excellent, but it's not the same. The partnership a rider builds with his horse, it's special, almost…"

He had a dreamy look on his face. "Do not say you're in love with your horse," I said.

The corner of his mouth turned up and he squeezed where he was holding my hips. "No, not quite. But *you* ride, I'm sure you get it."

I did, but it was fun to tease him. I scrunched up my face. "Yeah, well. Don't be *that* guy, Brady. Don't be the guy who loves his horse too much."

The smile dissolved from his face as he said, "I won't, Brooklyn. I promise." Which sounded like he was responding to something more than my lame joke. He looked at me then, intense like before, his eyes holding mine as he seemed to search my soul. Overwhelmed by it, I broke the gaze, looking over his shoulder, willing my heart to stop pounding.

The song began to mix into a fast one and I realized we'd

117

danced for not one, but two slow songs.

"Thanks, Brady," I said as we stepped apart.

"Tomorrow at eleven?" he asked as we walked toward my friends.

I nodded. "Yes. Thank you."

"Brooklyn," he said, stopping me in my tracks before we got to the edge of the dance floor.

"Yeah?"

"Thanks for dancing with me. If you'll notice," he paused, moving only his eyes toward the group of faculty, but not his head, not even a twitch. "The dean has her eyes on me, so I can't ask you to dance again tonight. But I want you to know it's not because I don't want to."

And with that, he left me.

Jared

The only thing holding me up two and a half hours later, long after Brady had left the gym, was the caffeine I'd ingested thanks to several sodas, and the resultant trips to the restroom. I was too tired physically to dance and too drained emotionally to care that I was standing by myself while my friends sucked every moment of joy they could out of their evening at Westwood.

"How you doing?" Kaylee asked from my left, startling me.

"Kaylee," I said. "When did you get back from the bathroom?"

She gave me an amused, wide-eyed look. "Twenty minutes ago. You asleep standing up there, Brooklyn?"

I exhaled. "Yes. Pretty much. Sorry I'm not very good company tonight."

"It's okay. You've had a rough week. And anyway, it's been a good night; I'm just standing here sort of reliving it. Which seems lame, but I don't care."

I looked at her and smiled. "We did both dance with hot guys, huh?"

She smiled back. "We did. I mean, it was kind of crazy how it happened, but yeah. And Declan..." she fanned her face, loudly blowing out a breath.

Laughing, I looked out at the crowd again, trying to find him. "Where did he go? He didn't leave early, did he?"

She shook her head. "No. He's over there with the guys."

I looked back out on the dance floor where a bunch of guys were fast dancing. "Why aren't you out there with them?"

Kaylee shrugged. "I'm not much of a fast dancer. And anyway, I didn't want to seem desperate. This kind of thing doesn't come easily to me, in case you hadn't noticed. I'm not Chelly."

Speaking of which... I glanced out and easily found

Seychelles in her siren red dress. She was in the middle of the dance floor, again, surrounded by guys like moths to her flame. "Wow. She really knows how to work it," I said, watching her laugh and interact with the boys like she was having the best time of her life. She probably was, I told myself.

"Amazing, isn't it?" Kaylee said, as awed as I was. "She makes it look so effortless."

"I think it *is* effortless for her. She's just one of those girls that oozes confidence. I mean, look around: she doesn't have the best body or the best hair, and I'm not trying to be mean at all, she just…"

"She's got it all," Kaylee finished, nodding. "That confidence is everything. Not too many people could even pull off that dress, but she totally owns it."

"So who's *she* after?" I tried to watch and see if she paid any special attention to any of the guys in particular, but she seemed to be an equal-opportunity flirter.

"I've never seen her date one guy exclusively."

I frowned at Kaylee. "Really?"

"Nope. Not for lack of offers. I mean, look at those guys sniffing around her. She's just a free spirit, I guess."

I looked back at Chelly, a little bit envious. Not that I wanted to be at the center of a group of guys who seemed to all want me. *Right.* Who was I trying to kid? "Wow. She's kind of living the dream."

Kaylee leaned into me and nudged me with her shoulder. "You know it, sister."

Scanning the crowd, I saw Emmie and Celia dancing among a group of guys also. Dave was right there with Emmie and I felt a huge pang of guilt and looked away from them.

"What about Celia? She got her eye on anyone?"

Kaylee looked out toward her roommate and shrugged. "She was into Steve Collins last year, but he's so busy with football and she's got her basketball practice…And," she added, leaning closer to me. "Between us, her academics aren't great. She needs to spend more time on studying or she's going to end up on notice by the dean."

I nodded, but was still curious what kind of guy Celia'd be into. "Is Steve here?"

She took a drink from her soda, but her eyes scanned the crowd. "Up in the bleachers. Short brown hair, no neck—your typical football jock."

That described four of the guys on the bleachers.

"The one on the end," Kaylee added, obviously reading my mind.

"And you?"

She looked at me. "And me, what?"

"You seemed to have a nice time dancing with Dylan."

"Declan," she corrected. "And I did. He's sweet."

"And hot," I added.

"So hot," she agreed. "So..."

"Irish? Tall? Nice?"

Kaylee turned to me and grinned. "The list goes on and on, doesn't it?"

"It does. If you ask me, which you didn't, but I'm going to pretend you did anyway, he's a way better choice than that Phillip douche."

She sighed. "I know. But Phillip, I don't know, there's something about him."

"Yes. He's an asshole."

"Exactly. Why do we like the wrong boys?"

I looked out at the crowd, my eyes landing on Dave. "I have no idea."

It wasn't much later that the DJ announced the last set of songs for the night. "Thank God," I muttered, glad that we'd be out of there and on the bus in ten minutes or so. I was desperate for my bed.

But then, as I was about to turn to Kaylee and let her know I was going to take one more trip to the restroom, I saw a guy coming straight for me, his eyes trained on me like I was a deer and he was a cougar. I swallowed and felt like I should turn and run, but that was ridiculous, and anyway, I didn't have time to move away.

It was the guy Dave had been talking to earlier when Emmie'd introduced me as her roommate. He seemed older than the other guys, but it had to be because he was bigger, with broader shoulders, and had dark, swarthy stubble and the long tied-back hair—though his green eyes still seemed very young. Something about him was familiar, but I was sure I'd never met him before—I'd definitely remember meeting this guy.

And then he was there in front of me, just inside my personal space, making me back up into the pillar behind me. He was so tall that I had to lean back to look up at his face. He smelled amazing, like the most perfect musk cologne had mingled with his own smell, enveloping my senses as I stood there. But more demanding of my attention was that he was standing there, smiling mischievously, making me no longer feel like prey, but more like a soon-to-be co-conspirator in some sort of plot.

Somehow, in something like four seconds, this guy had me completely and utterly intrigued.

And breathless.

"Hi," he said, his voice deep and smooth. "Brooklyn, right?"

Wow. I nodded, my brain unable to access words at that very moment.

"Dance?" he asked, holding out his hand.

I glanced over at Kaylee, who gave me an encouraging look, which was all I needed. I nodded again and slid my hand into the boy's.

"I'm Abe," he said as we walked out to the dance floor.

"Nice to meet you," I forced out of my mouth. And then thought of all the other Westwood guys I'd met, not wanting any other misunderstandings. I looked at him sideways. "Wait, first name or last name?"

He gave me a confused look as we stopped at an empty spot

on the floor. He put his big, warm hands on me, but he was so tall they landed not on my waist, but on my sides, right over my bra. I tried to put that fact out of my brain, but blushed fiercely anyway.

He tilted his head. "So, you don't know?"

Don't know what? I smiled at him. "I'm the new girl, so you can assume I don't know anything." I couldn't reach around his neck comfortably, so I held onto the backs of his biceps, my forearms supported by his arms. I tried not to get distracted by how muscular he was. Not an easy task, but I tried to focus on his pink pocket square at my eye level, realizing quickly that if I stayed focused on his face, I was going to finish the dance with a very sore neck.

He turned his head like he was surveying the rest of the couples on the dance floor and then blew out a breath. "I'm Jared Abromovich, but you probably would know me as Abrams."

My brain stuttered for a moment as it tried to compute: Jared Abrams.

And then it clicked. "From that show *Lady Parts*?"

He nodded, his smile faltering a little and I suddenly felt bad. Jared Abrams had been a child actor. At one time, he was the *it* kid of network TV, starring in that really popular sitcom about two women who ran an automotive garage; he was one of the women's kids. He'd grown up on that show and I even remembered some episodes in about the fifth season when his voice changed and cracked all the time—it had to be so hard growing up in the spotlight. As my hands barely circled halfway around his arms, he hardly looked like little Ricky from the show anymore. I had to think that wasn't an accident.

"Is it better or worse if I tell you I loved the show?" I asked.

He shrugged. "I'm used to it, so neither."

"Well, for what it's worth, I did love it and thought you especially were great. You got robbed at the Golden Globes that year."

He smiled as he looked down at me. "That's what my mom

123

said, but she might be biased."

"She's totally right," I said. "And I'm not at all biased. I mean come on, you're the fifth child actor I've hung out with this week alone—I don't play favorites. So you can totally trust me."

His smile widened, making his eyes crinkle in a very sexy way. It seemed the new and improved, completely exhausted Brooklyn who was too tired to be shy or concerned about what she said, was a hit at this dance.

"Thanks," he said softly, validating I'd said exactly the right thing.

"So the guys call you Abe?" I asked lamely.

So much for that conversational hot streak.

He nodded. "So, tell me about you," he said. "You're quite the novelty around here, being the new girl."

I blushed, feeling weird that the guys were talking about me. Although it's not like it was something I could complain about to Jared (or, I guess, *Abe*, but calling guys by their last names seemed like such a...guy thing, I guess) who'd been in the spotlight for many years.

"There's not much to say," I said.

"What about your family? Where are you from?"

That was kind of a loaded question that I couldn't really answer, so I told him about my time in London. Then he told me about a press junket he did around the premiere of a movie he had a tiny part in that took him to London, too. I didn't want to seem starstruck, but his story was really interesting and his delivery was great; he's really funny and a natural story-teller.

By the time the songs wound down and the lights came on in the gym, making us squint and mutter angrily, I'd come to realize I didn't want the dance to end, despite my earlier desire for my bed. Jared was good company and I'd wished he'd asked me to dance earlier.

"Thanks," I said sincerely.

"My pleasure. It was great to get to know you, Brooklyn. I have a feeling we're going to see each other again soon." He gave me another one of those mischievous smiles and a sexy little wink that made my stomach lurch. Especially when I realized he was still holding me. His hands tightened on me a little—it was kind of making me dizzy.

"I'll be here next week to work with Dave on the inter-school projects. Maybe then," I said, stepping back out of his grasp and giving him what I hoped was a matching smile, though I couldn't bring myself to wink.

"Looking forward to it."

"Come on, Brooklyn," Celia said from behind me as she came up and looped her arm through mine. "The bus is leaving. Later, Abe." She gave him a wave over her shoulder as she tugged me toward the door.

"He is super hot, so I get it," she said quietly. "But what about Brady?"

"Brady wasn't here to ask her to dance at the end," Kaylee said as she materialized on the other side of me. "Abe asked her. Nothing wrong with dancing with him, too. Two hot guys, huh, Brooklyn?" She waggled her eyebrows at me.

I didn't say it out loud, but actually, Jared made three hot guys I'd danced with that night.

Even surrounded by a bus full of excited, chattering girls, I fell asleep on the way back to Rosewood. Kaylee had to wake me up and practically drag me up to my room while the other girls hung out in the lounge, rehashing the entire evening. Had I not been nearly comatose, I'd have joined them, but my brain just wouldn't allow it.

And also, if I'd been conscious enough to identify it, I was nervous about being around Emmie; that dance with Dave had been awkward. Way awkward. And although I didn't have a lot (okay: any) experience with guys, there had been something in the way he'd looked at me and I was terrified she'd seen it, too.

I'd been at Rosewood for two weeks and although everyone

had been nice, the last thing I wanted to do was upset anyone, especially my roommate, the girl who had already done so much for me.

Once I got in our room and the door closed behind me, I unzipped Emmie's dress and let it slip off my shoulders. I hung it up as I kicked off my shoes, moaning in relief as I did. I used the bathroom and swiped a damp Kleenex over my face to remove at least some of my makeup.

Then I fell into bed.

It had been both the most awkward and kind of the best night of my life. I had danced with three cute guys was my last conscious thought as I drifted off to sleep.

Only to be awakened not ten minutes later.

Burgled

"**B**rooklyn!" Emmie hollered, maybe for the first time, maybe for the seventh—I don't know. All I knew was that she woke me up from a dead sleep.

And I was not impressed.

I rolled away toward the wall, prepared to ignore her until I could get back to sleep.

But one thing about Emmie that should come as no surprise by now? She would not be ignored.

"Brooklyn, you have to wake up. Seriously."

And then it hit me that maybe she'd come to grill me about Dave. I turned and looked up at her, blinking away the cobwebs, even though I'd only been asleep for a few minutes.

She didn't look mad. Actually, she was grinning; whatever it was, it wasn't about Dave.

Relieved, I closed my eyes and mumbled something. Even I couldn't tell what I'd intended to say.

She barked my name again and my brain finally clued in that I should just get whatever this was over with. I sat up and looked at her. She was holding out a printed card.

"What?" I whined.

"Look. Did you not see this when you came back?"

I narrowed my burning eyes. "See what?"

She shook it toward me. "This."

"Not helping, Emmie."

My roommate sighed and dropped to the edge of my bed. "You didn't notice your underwear drawer was open and this was on top?"

Okay, *that* got my attention. I took the card and squinted at it.

Dear Panty Owner, a pair of your underthings has been borrowed for the evening. Thank you.
To receive them back, you must go to the rear door of the Rosewood aquatic center, Saturday evening at 10:45 p.m.
Signed, TWPP*

*The Westwood Panty Posse

I looked up at Emmie. "What does this mean?"

She rolled her eyes. "Panty raid, Brooklyn. They snuck in here while we were on our way to the dance and stole our panties."

I looked around the room. Nothing had seemed out of place when I'd returned from the dance, but of course, I'd been focused on getting into bed as quickly as possible. "They were here? Wait...who?"

"The boys. Did you notice their pocket squares?"

It took me several long seconds to get it. And then, as Emmie stood there, watching me, her face pulled up in a smirk, like I'd seen on all those guys earlier...

"NO!" I said. "They were wearing our underwear as *pocket squares*?"

She tapped my nose. "Right you are, Sherlock."

"Did you know this?"

She shook her head. "Not until we got back here. We aren't the only ones with notes. Those rotten boys. I'm going to kill Dave." But she hardly looked mad. She actually looked...giddy?

"So his orange pocket square?"

"One of my thongs."

I looked down at the card still in my hand. Which meant...I swallowed. "And Jared's pink one?"

Emmie pointed at my underwear drawer, still ajar. "Yours, I bet."

128

"Oh. My. God. Are you serious?"

She nodded her head toward my open drawer before turning to go use the bathroom. "See for yourself," she said over her shoulder.

But it wasn't the missing panties that had me suddenly moving like I had a fire under my butt.

I swung my legs out of bed and jumped up. Digging in my underwear drawer, pushing my panties aside, trying not to think about boys going through all of my underwear (especially my torn, old 'that time of the month' ones) my fingers grasped the box tucked away at the back. Pulling it out, I held my breath and prayed silently that what was inside hadn't been discovered.

But as I opened it and saw the inner compartment was still locked, I sighed in relief, thankful that all the boys got from me was a stupid pair of underwear. Glancing back at the bathroom, not wanting Emmie to see the box, I slipped it back into the drawer, surrounding it with socks and then rearranging the underwear which had been scattered by who knew how many boys' hands.

"Why would they do that?"

Emmie came out of the bathroom that second, stripped down to her bra and panties. "What?"

I shook my head. "I was just wondering why they would steal our underwear?"

"Silly, Brooklyn. It's obvious: because they're *boys* and they want our attention."

"Mission accomplished."

"And I have to admit, the pocket square thing is brilliant — that none of them let on all night? Hilarious."

I had to agree, although it was a little embarrassing if I really thought about it. "How many were in on it?"

She shook her head. "Not sure, but we got hit, Kaylee and Celia, Debbie and Sarah next door, Chelly and Naomi…most of the girls on our floor."

"So just juniors?" I thought about all the boys who had pocket squares at the dance. There had been quite a few. With

129

the exception of Brady, of course.

"Yeah. Dave and his friends. Not sure which one would have been the mastermind, though."

"I guess Brady's not friends with them?"

"Not really," Emmie said with a frown.

"Did something happen?"

"What do you mean?" she asked.

"Like to make them not like him or something."

She blinked and then her eyes widened like she thought I was upset about them not being friends.

"Oh no, it's not like that. They like him and all. He's just...I don't know, a bit of a loner type. Like I said before, kind of broody, intense. And *way* too mature to sneak in here and steal panties."

She gave me a look, but I could tell she kind of loved the attention. "Children," she muttered, not fooling anyone.

"So now what? And more importantly, can I please get back into bed?"

She waved toward my bed and I crawled back in under the sheets.

"We're not going to play into their game. Oh no..." she said with an evil smirk worthy of any good supervillain. All she was missing was the maniacal laughter.

"What does that mean?"

"It means I'm leaving to go back to the lounge and the other girls; I'll fill you in tomorrow. You look like the walking dead."

I wanted to know what she had planned, but I *felt* like the walking dead, so I wasn't even offended she'd said it. Grateful to be dismissed, I nodded at her and turned over, asleep in seconds.

$\mathcal{S}$aturday $\mathcal{P}$ractice

I woke up in a panic, terrified I'd overslept and would be late for my lesson with Brady. But a glance at the clock told me I had plenty of time: it was only 8:30.

I stretched, extending my arms over my head until I could push against the wall, and although some of my muscles still ached from overuse, overall I felt better. Maybe my body was getting used to the abuse.

Which made me think of today's practice with Brady. Which made me think of *Brady* and dancing with him the night before.

Which made me shiver because, well, because he was sexy and intense and looked amazing in his riding breeches.

And then there was the fact that the girls seemed to think he was into me. If I allowed myself to think about it as though it was happening to someone else, I had to admit I thought so, too.

But then, as I rehashed the rest of the evening, I thought about dancing with Dave, which had been so complicated and awkward, but secretly thrilling, too. Especially when I'd caught him looking at me, like something was going on. Or maybe that he *wanted* something to go on. Even if nothing could ever happen with my roommate's boyfriend and I would never let it, it was still secretly exciting to think maybe he was into me a little.

And then there was Jared, the former child actor who was now a big and very masculine guy, who, as all the events of the evening really started coming back to me, I remembered was currently holding my panties hostage.

That made me smile and blush at the same time. I wondered what we were going to do to get them back. I glanced over at Emmie, but she was still fast asleep, probably tweaking her evil plot in her dreams. Sure she was up late with the other girls, I got out of bed quietly so as not to wake her, and tiptoed to the bathroom.

~ ♥ ~

There wasn't enough time to really start in on any of my homework, so, although I'd be early, I got dressed for riding, plunked my helmet over my braid, and left my dorm room, leaving Emmie to sleep in. I grabbed some food on my way out to the stables, including an apple and some carrots for Charlie. I figured I'd take an extra half-hour or so to warm up and practice before Brady arrived.

Brady.

Thinking about him as I got Charlie saddled up, my heart sped up a little, and although I could try to deny out loud that he'd had any effect on me, obviously my body knew otherwise. That realization made me feel a bit dizzy.

Brady. Very cute guy who was also into horses.

And was my teacher. Ugh.

No, I corrected myself; my *coach.* Who was less than a year older than me. I mean, if he had just been another student helping me out with my dressage practice, I wouldn't think it was weird if we started dating. It wasn't like he was forty and divorced or anything. He was just a senior: *totally* eligible for dating.

Dating. My hand shook a little as I fastened the bridle on Charlie. I'd never really dated anyone. I'd barely even been kissed. Was I ready to do all that now?

Definitely.

"And why not?" I asked Charlie.

Charlie had no objections, so I gave him a friendly pat, finished getting him ready and walked him to the arena, laughing as he nudged me along with his nose. When I got there, the big door was already open and I realized quickly I wasn't the first to arrive.

Brady was there already. He was riding Sir Lancelot, by the looks of it, around the arena that was set up with a series of jumps. I'd done some jumping back when I'd started lessons, but nothing over a two foot cavaletti. These jumps looked taller than me and had to be at, or at least very near, Olympic height. He circled the outside of the ring in a controlled canter, looking like he was glued to the horse by his thighs and seat.

I'd never seen Brady ride, since he conducted his lessons standing in the ring. But as I watched him, all I could think of was that phrase *poetry in motion*.

Because that's exactly what was in front of me. Pure equestrian perfection.

And then he pulled Sir Lancelot in to start the course.

I held my breath as they approached the first jump, and then let it out as they soared over it. They approached the next and my breath caught again.

They cleared it without even a nick of the hoof.

The way he cantered around the ring taking jump after jump so effortlessly, it appeared he and the horse were one being.

"Wow," I whispered aloud as I watched, stunned by how Brady took the intensity that was such a part of him and turned it toward jumping a clear round. His eyes never wavered from the course, seemingly always a jump ahead. I wondered if he competed in show jumping, too.

Finally, he finished the round and slowed, weaving around the jumps as he walked his horse. His ride, though seeming effortless, left him breathing heavy, his chest rising and falling as he caught his breath.

He noticed me then and my heart fluttered as his face spread into a smile and he walked Sir Lancelot over to us.

Charlie nickered a greeting, returned by a whinny from Sir Lancelot. Funny how horses could be so open with their greetings, yet I was suddenly feeling very shy and a bit flustered as Brady approached.

"Hi," he said, dismounting. He took a step toward me and then glanced at his horse, the one he'd told me had been dubbed *Sir Bitesalot*. He stayed where he was and I kept my distance.

"Hey. I thought you were training this morning."

133

"My coach is sick. She canceled."

She? Why did that suddenly make me very jealous? *Don't be ridiculous,* I told myself. *It's not like he's even yours. Just because you thought about dating him, doesn't mean it's even going to happen.* "Do you show jump?" I asked.

He was looking at me strangely, like he wanted to say something, but was holding back for some reason. He shook his head. "Just to let off steam sometimes," he said, the last trace of his smile gone now.

I wondered what had suddenly changed. He'd seemed happy to see me at first, but now, he was reserved, uptight.

"You're very good," I said. Not trying to flatter him, but because it was the truth and I wanted him to know I'd noticed.

"Thanks."

A silence stretched between us. An awkward silence.

"I thought he was a biter," I said, nodding toward Sir Lancelot, figuring anything would be better than more silence.

"He's okay with me," Brady said. And then blushed, looking away.

Why was he blushing? And why did it make him seem even more attractive? "What's wrong?" I blurted out.

He looked at me sideways. "He only bites girls."

I laughed. "Charming."

Brady smiled. "I know. He's a crabby old guy, but he's fun to jump." He swallowed, his Adam's apple moving up and down in his neck.

There was another long silence.

Brady finally broke it. "Well, I should get Lance back. Why don't you take Charlie to the outside ring today so those jumps aren't in our way? Don't get on him until I get back, okay? I won't be long."

"I was going to warm up," I said. "That's why I came early."

He shook his head. "You can't—students aren't allowed to ride without an instructor present. It's an insurance thing."

"Oh," I said. "Okay, I'll just walk over and meet you there, then."

He nodded and walked away, not looking back.

~ ❤ ~

It wasn't long before he returned, but it felt like long enough for an eternity's worth of doubts to form and start swirling in my head. Had I imagined that he liked me? Had my friends? Had I done something wrong? What had changed?

I stood there with Charlie, petting his velvet nose, trying to absorb his quiet calm to help ease my jangling nerves.

It worked a little, until Brady returned, striding toward the outdoor arena, looking amazingly sexy in his riding outfit. Suddenly, like he was on a mission, he walked straight up to me. His eyes burned into mine and when he didn't stop a few feet away, I began to panic.

Because I was suddenly sure he was going to grab me and kiss me.

My lungs froze on a breath. My heart began to race.

And then he stopped right in front of me, inside my bubble and close enough that I could smell him; leather, saddle soap, boy.

I looked up at him. His lips were turned up in a slight smile and then they parted. He reached up toward my face, his eyes taking me in with his usual intensity. My cheeks flushed, but ached for his touch. I licked my dry lips and swallowed, suddenly worried about too much saliva. I did not want to ruin this kiss. My eyes fluttered closed as he leaned in.

He cleared his throat. "You have to do this up," he said.

My eyes popped open. "What?"

And then I realized he wasn't reaching for my face, but for the straps of my riding helmet, bringing them together under my chin. Clicking them into place.

Oh. My. God.

It wasn't a kiss; it was a safety precaution.

I wanted to die.

Except I couldn't; I still had two hours of practice with him.

135

Counterplot

I never did get to soak in the whirlpool like I'd hoped. And it's not because I didn't need it after practice with Brady, either. He worked me extra hard and I seriously questioned whether he'd blown off enough steam with his morning ride or maybe he was taking something out on me. Still, I was relieved that when we got into the ring, he put on his Coach Fleming hat and was all business; I didn't have time to think about the almost kiss that wasn't.

Thank God.

After that, I'd grabbed some lunch and headed back to my dorm room to get my bathing suit when Emmie told me we needed to meet the other girls in less than half an hour. "I'm just finishing up this e-mail to my mother and then we can head down the hall," she said, her back to me.

"I'm going to wash the stables off me," I said, heading into the bathroom.

When I emerged from my shower, Emmie was standing in front of our shared closet. She looked over her shoulder at me. "Did you like that dress you wore last night?"

"Yeah. Thanks again for lending it to me."

She waved me off and pulled the dress in question out of the closet, holding it up. "Do you want it?"

Was she offering me her designer dress? "You mean, to keep?"

She nodded. "Yes. I'm selling a bunch of dresses, but if you want this one, I won't."

I hardly thought she was hurting for money, but I couldn't take her dress. "It's nice, but no, you go ahead."

"You're sure?"

I nodded.

She smiled. "Okay. It's for a good cause and that dress will probably bring in three or four goats."

"Goats?"

"Yeah, there's a charity where you can buy people in less privileged countries stuff from a catalog, like a goat or chickens or water pumps and stuff. It's a smart way for them to itemize donations so people feel like they're giving something tangible. It's kind of a crock, but the money still goes where it's needed."

"And you're selling your fancy clothes to donate?"

She shrugged like it was no big deal. "It's my personal *Gucci to Goats* program."

I laughed.

But her smile faded when she said, "My parents are so bourgeois, they will think nothing of buying a four thousand dollar dress for their daughter, but wouldn't give one penny to a needy charity. It's disgusting, really. But I do my part. I just e-mailed my mother, telling her I needed some gowns to choose from for the Halloween dance. Wait until you see what she sends in a week or so."

All I could do was stare at my roommate in awe.

"What?"

I shook my head. "You're going to run the world someday."

She winked. "Probably."

All the girls who'd had their panties 'borrowed' were assembled in the lounge, sitting at the round tables and chatting, speculating on what we were going to do next. There were fourteen of us in all—like Emmie said, just from our floor; we knew Dave and his friends were behind the prank, but not how many of them were involved. We assumed fourteen, but it was hard to know for sure.

Kaylee and Celia sat with me at a table as I tried to catch up on my French homework. They were discussing the upcoming English Lit paper, which was almost identical to one I'd done back in London, so I was going to be a good environmentalist and recycle for that, but the French assignment was new.

Our fearless leader, Emmie of course, breezed in and took her spot at the front of the room beside the microwave and fridge. I closed up my textbook, not that I was getting much done anyway.

"Hi girls," she said, causing a hush to come over us. "So, let's get right to it. I think everyone got one of the note cards saying that we're supposed to be behind the aquatics center tonight. Anyone get anything different?" she scanned the crowd, but no one spoke up.

She continued. "So my assumption is that they wanted to do a prank to get our attention."

"Uh, yeah. And it worked," Celia said. We all laughed.

"Yes, but we're not going to play their little game. Now they want us to meet up with them, laugh and stroke their egos and tell them how clever they are."

Glancing at some of the girls around me and taking in their expressions, I got the impression they were okay with that. It was, after all, a pretty clever prank, especially the pocket square thing. And any opportunity to hang out with the boys was a welcome one.

"What do you mean?" Celia asked.

"I say we do something unexpected. Show them they can't just come in here and steal our underwear."

"What do you have in mind?" Naomi, Chelly's roommate, asked.

A slow smile spread across Emmie's face. "I want to give them a taste of their own medicine."

There was a second of silence as everyone processed this, until Chelly whooped. "GOTCHIE RAID!"

There were a few gasps and lots of laughs, but then everyone started talking at once.

"How do we know whose to steal?" Celia asked.

"We can't know exactly who's involved, but I suspect whoever asked you to dance last night for the last song, is the guy who has your underwear." She pointed at me. "Start a list, will you, Brooklyn? Everyone write down who you danced with."

"Wait, we'll still get to see the guys, though, won't we?" Chelly asked, obviously not wanting to give up a chance to meet up with some boys.

Emmie rolled her eyes, which was funny, since I knew she wouldn't give up an opportunity to meet up with Dave, but she said, "Yes, Chelly. But we're not just going to steal their underwear; we're going to do this right and on our terms. Isn't that better?"

"I don't care," she said, "They can keep my panties and take ten more pairs, for all I care, as long as I get some action tonight." That caused an eruption of laughter.

I tore a blank sheet out of my notebook and wrote Jared's name at the top and then passed it to Kaylee, who wrote down Declan's name. I had been so wrapped up in dancing with Jared, I hadn't even noticed she'd ended the night with him.

I was about to ask her how it had gone when she looked over at me, suddenly horror-stricken. "We can't do this," she whispered. "We could get expelled."

"Really? Expelled over an underwear raid? That seems pretty harsh."

She shook her head. "It's not about the underwear; we'd be leaving campus."

Right. Leaving the Rosewood campus was a definite no-no. I could hardly blame Kaylee for being reluctant when the stakes were so high. I wondered if Emmie had thought of this. "Do you think it's such a good idea to leave campus?" I asked. "I mean, won't we get busted for leaving Rosewood?"

She crossed her arms over her chest and looked quite smug when she said, "If we left on our own, sure. That's why we're going to get the dean to drive us."

Counterplot Execution

I had to admit, once she explained it, Emmie's plan was pretty good. Sure, there were ways we could get busted, like if we got caught up in the guys' dorms, or somehow the dean figured out my backpack suddenly contained boys' underwear. But if that happened it would be a misdemeanor and result in us getting a talking to—nothing close to getting expelled. And, Emmie explained, they only called home for major things, since most busy parents who shipped their kids off to Rosewood did so because they didn't want to be bothered with day to day school stuff like silly school pranks, and trusted the Rosewood administration to handle regular non-life-threatening teenage behavior. So the chance of our parents finding out, if we did get caught, was very slim.

So it looked like the first part of her plan was fairly low risk and I did appreciate that. The second part—the part that she had stayed up until almost five a.m. to set up, was pure brilliance.

My only complaint was that Emmie was including me in it as her one and only co-conspirator for the first part. But it was also flattering that she trusted me, and maybe it meant she was really okay with that whole Dave thing and wasn't holding a grudge or anything.

And anyway, I wasn't about to chicken out. Girls who want to fit in don't chicken out on stuff like this. And the new Brooklyn really wanted to fit in.

This was the first part of her plan as she explained it to us: As the school liaison, she knew that Dean Haywood had dinner with Westwood's Dean Peterson every Saturday to discuss...well, whatever it was deans discussed about their respective schools. She thought maybe it was a hookup, but whatever it was, it meant Dean Haywood would be traveling to Westwood in just a couple of hours. Emmie was going to go to the dean and suggest that she and I go with her on today's trip. That way, Emmie would reason, she could hand over her school liaison duties to me as I'd be taking over the following week, and she'd be able to formally introduce me to Westwood's dean and school liaison (Dave) and help me familiarize myself with the school and their procedures. She was going to stress how necessary this orientation would be, especially for one new to the school, such as myself.

Then, during the deans' closed door meeting in the Westwood offices, we'd steal the boys' underwear while they were at dinner.

Simple.

Though simple didn't mean completely bulletproof.

But like I said, I wasn't about to chicken out, so two hours later and after some fancy talking by Emmie, we were in the dean's nondescript sedan, driving over to Westwood.

Thankfully, Emmie sat in the front passenger seat and easily chatted with the dean about her summer in Europe.

I sat in the back, getting more and more nervous. No matter how many times I smoothed my sweaty palms over my kilt, they just got clammy again.

Until, "Ms. Prescott, I understand your dressage is coming along nicely."

I glanced up at the rear view mirror; the dean's eyes were on me. I nodded. "Yes, thank you. Coach Fleming has been really helpful."

"I also saw you dancing with him last night."

Okay. "Yes, that's right."

"May I remind you he's faculty."

Huh? "I beg your pardon?"

Her eyes darted up to the mirror again. "His coaching you is not an invitation to *hook up*, as you kids call it."

There was no way to hide the blush on my cheeks. But I wasn't sure if I was blushing because she was onto me or because she'd just mentioned a *hookup*. "No ma'am," I choked out.

"And just to make sure, I've said as much to him. I don't need my stables used as a brothel."

Emmie snorted and then covered it up with a cough.

The dean looked over at her. "Something wrong, Ms. Somerville?"

"No, ma'am. Just a tickle in my throat."

But wait, the dean had spoken to Brady? About us using the stables as a *brothel*? Oh my God, I was never going to be able to look him in the eye again. As though I hadn't been humiliated enough by that almost kiss that was most definitely *not* an almost kiss.

I felt like I should say something, but my brain seemed to be uninterested in joining the conversation in any coherent way. And really, what could I possibly say? *Brothel?* Really?

"Ma'am," Emmie said, coming to my rescue. "I can assure you that Brooklyn has not used the stables or any other location on the Rosewood grounds in any such way. Her relationship with Coach Fleming is strictly professional."

"It's true," I said, thankful to Emmie for getting the ball rolling. "Our relationship is purely professional." *Especially since he's obviously not interested,* I didn't say out loud. "When we danced last night, he was just being friendly."

I kicked Emmie's seat when she snorted again. At least this time, she was quieter about it.

I saw Dean Haywood's knuckles begin to loosen up on the wheel; she must not have heard the snort. "Well that is what he said when I spoke with him last night, but I'm happy to hear the same from you as well."

Ugh. So she had already spoken to him about this when we had our practice? No wonder he was so weird. And maybe it explained why he'd seemed to lose his feelings for me.

If he ever had any in the first place.

As the conversation drifted to other topics (thank you again, Emmie) I looked out the window and tried to figure out what I could possibly say to Brady now that things were going to be so awkward between us.

A few minutes later, we pulled up to Westwood and the dean pulled into one of the marked visitors' parking spots out front. I got out and looked up at the building that seemed so different than it had just last night. Amazing how much can change in one day.

"Let's go, girls," Dean Haywood said after she got out of her car. As we fell in line behind her, I looked at Emmie. She nodded back and I took it to mean something like *'stay cool'* and *'I've got this'*. At least, that's what I *hoped* she meant. I was way out of my league on this underwear thieving expedition.

~💙~

Eight minutes later, after some super-smooth talking from Emmie (she was so convincing, *I* almost believed her story) we were on our own, sneaking down some back service hallway of Westwood. I'd met Dean Peterson and then Emmie had told them we were off to meet up with Dave, so he and I could officially meet—although Dean Haywood had remembered quite clearly that I'd danced with Brady, she seemed not to have noticed that I'd also danced with Dave. Meeting with Dave was the weak link in our plan—he didn't even know we were on campus. Emmie assured me it was a non-issue, but it felt like a dangerously loose thread to me.

"How do you know where we're going?" I asked.

She shot me a look over her shoulder. "Please. When you are the liaison and you have a boyfriend here, you find the unused hallways."

"For what?"

She rolled her eyes. "Um, making out?"

"Right," I said, feeling stupid.

Emmie shrugged and kept walking. "It's not like we can sneak up to his room. He has a roommate, and if we got caught with me up there…"

She didn't need to finish her sentence; surely Westwood had strict rules about entertaining members of the opposite sex in

143

dorm rooms. In a few minutes we got to a set of back stairs and started up them to the second floor. "Do you know where Dave's room is, though?"

"Yeah, look," she handed me a folded piece of paper from her pocket. It was a rough sketch of the building with stars in several locations—underwear targets, I figured. "They're on the second floor."

"You made a map?"

"Well, yeah. We don't have a lot of time. And I really would rather get in and out and then just go hang out by the Dean's office so the guys don't see us up here."

I wasn't arguing. "No, I think it's great. I'm totally impressed. So you're sure they're at dinner?"

She pulled out her phone and tapped the screen to wake it up. "Yeah. Dinner started like five minutes ago."

We got up to the second floor and she peeked out through the small window in the fire door. "Looks clear," she said, gently pushing the bar across the door to open it out to the hallway. We froze and listened, but the only sound was the buzz of the fluorescent overhead lights. And my blood rushing through my ears, but maybe only I could hear that.

"Let's go," she said, unnecessarily; I was eager to get this over with. Sure, it was exciting, but the idea of getting caught by a teacher, or maybe worse, one of the guys, was enough to get me into near panic mode. "We'll start with Dave's room—if we have to bolt, I want to make sure I at least have his."

I followed her down the hall to the third door on the right. She grabbed the knob, but it didn't budge: locked. I glanced at her face to see if this was going to be an impediment, but she just looked more focused as she dug around in her pants pocket and pulled out some sort of tiny screwdriver. She shoved it into the lock, jiggled it around and the next thing I knew, we were inside.

"You're amazing," I whispered, seriously impressed by my cat burglar of a roommate.

"I only use my powers for good." She waggled her eyebrows at me and nodded toward a dresser. "You get from there, I'll grab Dave's."

I glanced around the room, taking in the posters and other things that made the room feel very masculine. On the side where Emmie was focused hung posters of guitars and people playing them. In the corner was an actual guitar case. "Does he play?" I nodded toward the case.

"Yeah. He's pretty good, actually. But come on, Brooklyn, focus."

I took a last look at Dave's nightstand and saw a framed photo of the two of them together. They looked really happy. *They* are *happy*, I said to myself. Turning away, I looked toward the other side of the room.

"Whose is this?" I asked, quickly opening the drawers in the dresser, looking for the underwear.

"Abe, the guy who had yours."

"Well that's convenient," I muttered and looked up at the photos tacked on his wall. Upon closer inspection, I realized they were of him and other actors. And based on how young he looked, they were probably taken on the set of *Lady Parts*. Some of the photos were just of him.

Weird. "Kind of into himself, isn't he?"

"What?" Emmie asked.

"All these pictures are of him. Kind of conceited, no?"

She shook her head. "He's the least conceited guy I know. He hates those pictures, actually. He hates that time of his life."

I glanced back at the photos, confused. "So why..."

"Dave says he's writing his memoir and the pictures take him back to that place. He thought it was weird that he put up the pictures too, so he asked him about it. But seriously, we need to get out of here. Take a picture with your phone for later or something."

I refocused on Jared's underwear drawer "So what are we looking for, here? Tightie whities? Boxers, what?"

"You're overthinking it, just grab a pair and let's go."

I scanned over the drawer full of...well, drawers and grabbed a black pair of boxer-briefs. Maybe the idea was to embarrass the guys, but there was very little about these that was embarrassing: this pair probably looked way sexy on Jared and just thinking about his muscular body in his underwear had me blushing fiercely.

"Ha, look at these!" Emmie said. I turned; she was holding up a pair of leopard-print bikinis.

"Oh my God. Does he wear those?" I asked, my face growing even hotter.

She shrugged. "I have no idea, but they're hilarious. Turn around." I did, offering my back to her, and handed her the pair of Jared's so she could stuff both of them into the backpack over my shoulders.

Nodding at me, she said, "Come on, we have plenty more to get."

With a grin, I nodded back and followed her to the next room.

$\mathscr{S}uccess$

We managed to collect fifteen pairs of underwear (Emmie took two from Phillip, "just because he was such a douche to Kaylee") and get back down to the first floor completely undetected. We slipped into the women's bathroom, the same one Kaylee and I had chatted in the night before, and Emmie texted Dave to come meet us in the hall.

Within moments, there was a soft knock at the door. "Em?"

We left the restroom and I was surprised to see Dave wasn't alone: Jared was with him. And he was smiling down at me. His long hair was down around his shoulders and he wore a 'Property of Westwood Athletics' t-shirt that even had the size on the front: XXL. It was tight across his chest, but totally in a good way. He wore jeans, too; his outfit a stark contrast to the suit he'd been wearing the night before.

Thinking about what we'd just done, I looked away, terrified we'd be found out just by my guilty face. And then I suddenly wondered where my underwear was. I hadn't thought to look for it in his room, but it obviously wasn't out in the open. Maybe they were in one of his pockets…

Dave leaned down and wrapped his arms around Emmie, gathering her into a full frontal hug, "Hey," he said softly before he gave her a kiss. I turned toward Jared to not gawk and give them some privacy.

"So, hi," I said in as breezy a tone as I could muster, you know, as though I *didn't* have his underwear in my backpack.

"What are you girls doing here?" Jared asked casually.

"Emmie's showing me around since I'm taking over the school liaison thing next week."

"Why didn't you let me know," Dave said from behind me. "I would have given you the grand tour."

Emmie jumped in, "It was a last minute thing. We came over

with the dean and just finished up meeting with her and Dean Peterson. Why don't we show Brooklyn where the student council office is?"

But as I looked over at my roommate and took in the way she and Dave were looking at each other, I had a feeling maybe they wanted a few minutes alone. Or maybe I wanted to not be around them while they really started making out in the hallway: an event I felt was imminent.

"Hey," I said to Jared. "Why don't you show me?"

Jared glanced over at Dave and shrugged. "Sure. Come on."

"Meet us at the front office in fifteen, Brooklyn," Emmie said authoritatively, but her eyes said a quick *thank you*. I hoped she wasn't going to spill the beans on what we'd just done, but just before I turned away, she gave me the tiniest of head shakes. *Don't let on*, it said. I nodded back my understanding.

As I walked down the hall next to him, I thought about Jared and what Emmie had said about him hating his childhood and how he was now writing his memoir. I wondered if it was some sort of therapy for him. I also wondered how bad his childhood really was—there were plenty of horror stories about the lives of child actors out there, though I couldn't remember hearing much specifically about him. Not that I was going to ask, but still…

"So," he said. "That dance was sure fun, huh?"

I looked up at him. "Yeah."

He exhaled and then pushed his fingers through his long hair. "Sorry."

"What?"

"That was lame. Can we start again?"

I wasn't sure what he was talking about, so I nodded.

"Hi, Brooklyn," he said, smiling. "It's nice to see you again. I had a good time dancing with you last night."

I was about to thank him and tell him I'd enjoyed dancing with him, too, just as polite conversation would dictate, when the new Brooklyn decided to take a different tack.

"It's nice to see you, too. And I enjoyed dancing with you as well. Right up until I got back to my dorm and realized you'd

148

stolen my underwear."

"Oh, right. That."

I laughed. "That's all you have to say? *Oh, right?*"

He gave me a sheepish smile. "It was a good ice-breaker, though."

"So is, '*hi, my name is Jared or Abe or whatever, would you like to dance?*'"

"True enough; point taken," he said, laughing.

"You even could have led with that child actor thing; I'm sure that works on girls every time," I blurted out. And was instantly sorry when his smile dissolved. *Nice going, Brooklyn,* I berated myself. *You know he's sensitive about his childhood and there you go, throwing it in his face.*

"Sorry," I said, my eyes on the floor as we walked down the quiet hallway. "I didn't mean to…"

"No, it's okay. You're right anyway. It does work." But his voice had an edge to it and I knew it wasn't okay.

We stopped in the hallway and I realized we were outside our destination, the Student Council Boardroom. Before we went in, I looked up at him, right into his eyes. "Listen, I'm really sorry. That was stupid. I'd like a do-over. You got one, so I think it's only fair."

He clenched his jaw and then nodded, crossing his arms over his chest. "Make it good."

"Please. '*It was nice to see you and I enjoyed dancing with you*' is your definition of good?"

He didn't say anything but gave me a challenging nod.

"Fine," I said, looking up at the ceiling as I thought about something that would *really* ease the tension. Then it came to me and before I could reconsider, I pasted a pouty, doe-eyed look on my face and said. "How's this: 'I had a great time with you last night, too, Jared. Except that when I got back to my dorm, I realized my favorite panties were gone. So today, I just couldn't bring myself to wear any at all."

His eyes didn't move from mine, but he swallowed audibly.

I didn't even care that my face had to be the color of a

tomato, nor that it was an outright lie. None of that mattered.

His eyes slowly left mine and moved down my body toward my skirt. He swallowed again.

"Yeah," he said, clearing his throat as he reached for the doorknob. "That works."

We only had about ten minutes, so Jared gave me what he called the ten cent tour before leading me back to the administrative offices at the front of the building. The tour was secondary to spending time with my guide; he really was fun to be with and I absolutely got why he'd been such a star. He was charming and witty and I bet even off-screen he'd been a really funny and precocious kid.

We made no further mention of the underwear, but it was sort of an unspoken thing between us since there was supposed to be some sort of reunion later that night. Of course, he didn't know the half of it.

Emmie and Dave showed up a few minutes later and then without much more said, the boys left and we went into the office to see if the dean was ready to head back.

"You didn't say anything, did you?" Emmie asked as we watched them walk away.

"No. I mean, he knows that I know he stole my underwear, obviously. But why we're here? No."

"Good. Dave doesn't have a clue, either. This is going to be awesome."

I knew she was talking mostly about her plot, but if she was also referring to seeing the boys again later that night, I had to agree.

All Because of Duct Tape

When we returned from Westwood, it was already almost seven-thirty, so we headed straight to the third floor lounge. Emmie had texted Chelly to get the girls assembled there so we could quickly organize the second part of her plan.

We expected the girls to be excited. What we didn't expect was the cheering.

Emmie laughed and held up her hands. "Yes, okay, thanks everyone. Before you congratulate us, we have a lot of work to do."

And like the born leader she is, Emmie delivered the rest of her instructions to her ranks.

~♥~

"How are we supposed to attach it?" Kaylee whispered.

We were in the bushes behind the aquatics center, trying to set up a webcam with my phone, because Emmie was adamant that we should have video. I agreed, but it was proving to be a challenge. We needed to set it up so it was out of sight, but would still capture the whole thing on tape. It would have been a lot easier if it wasn't autumn and we could hide it behind some leaves instead of bare stems. "I don't know," I said, looking around for a better spot.

"What if we fix it to that tree, there," she said. "We could angle it so the camera has a clear shot, but have the phone behind a branch."

It was a good idea, but we didn't have anything to secure it with. "Wait," I said, remembering. "There's some duct tape in the stables. Why don't you run and grab it and I'll stay here and find the perfect angle. It's in the tack room on a peg just inside the door."

"Or, *you* could go and grab the tape, since you know where it is."

Yes, that makes more sense, but I really don't want to run into Brady, I didn't say. "Do you mind going?" I practically begged.

"Yes, Brooklyn, I do mind. Come on, we don't have a lot of time to get this set up. Just go."

I had no good argument, so I crouched and picked my way out of the bush, Kaylee right behind me. "And anyway," she said. "I saw Brady leave earlier. You probably won't run into him."

I gave her a look over my shoulder.

"Sorry," she said with a shrug. I'd told her on our way to the center what the dean had said and that she'd told Brady the same thing, so of course she'd know why I didn't want to go to the stables. "For what it's worth, I still think he's into you."

"Yeah, well, maybe he was, but not anymore." I wasn't so sure though. I'd probably imagined him ever being into me even a little.

I left Kaylee and walked quickly over to the stables. The door was closed but not locked, so I pushed it open, calling out, "Hello?"

Jerry, the stable hand popped his head around the corner. "Hi there, I'm getting ready to lock up for the night, did you forget something?"

"Oh hi," I said, thankful he wasn't Brady. "I was just hoping to borrow the duct tape—I saw some earlier."

Jerry jutted his chin toward the tack room. "Help yourself."

I jogged around the corner and grabbed the tape, yelling out a thank you as I slipped the roll over my wrist and headed back toward the door. But as I grabbed the handle and pulled, it moved toward me too quickly; someone was coming in. And they were in a hurry. The movement of the door knocked me off balance and before I could steady myself, I ended up on my butt on the concrete floor.

The pain took a second but then kicked in, radiating from my tail bone all the way to my toes.

"Brooklyn?"

I looked up. Of course it was Brady.

Perfect.

"I'm so sorry. Are you okay?" he reached for my hands and gently lifted me to my feet.

"Yeah," I breathed. "I just…it…ow." I hunched over a little, waiting out the pain. It seemed to lessen a bit as I did some yoga breathing.

"I'm so sorry. I got home and realized I forgot my phone and I…it doesn't matter…" he shook his head. "Are you okay?"

I nodded. And then realized he was still holding my hands. His were warm and big; strong riding hands. I quickly let them go.

"What's going on…?" Jerry poked his head around the corner again. "Oh, hey, Brady. You back for your phone?" before waiting for an answer, he dug in his shirt pocket and pulled out the phone in question, handing it over.

Brady took it. "Thanks. We'll get out of your hair so you can lock up." He turned to me. "C'mon," he said, grabbing my elbow and leading me slowly outside. The door closed and latched behind us.

"I'm okay," I said, suddenly eager to get away from him. "Thanks."

"What are you thanking me for? I just knocked you on your ass."

"I don't know," I said, looking at the ground.

"Brooklyn?"

"Yeah?"

"Look at me."

I'd really rather not, I thought. But I looked up at him anyway, noticing the shadows defining his cheekbones in the waning autumn dusk.

"What's wrong?"

Ugh. We are so not going there. "Nothing." I said.

"Why won't you look at me?"

I did then. "It's awkward."

He pushed a stray lock of my hair behind my ear, making me shiver. "Tell me," he said.

"The dean..."

He exhaled and looked away, combing his fingers through his hair. "She got to you, too?"

I nodded. "Listen, Brady, I don't know why she even thought..." I stopped talking because suddenly his hand was on my face, his thumb tracing my cheek.

"She thought it because it's true."

I stopped breathing.

"I like you, Brooklyn. But..." he sighed again and looked at the sky before returning his gaze to mine. "I can't. I can't jeopardize this job. I can't get involved. Not now. This is so not about you. Do you understand?"

"You're going to the Olympics. Of course I understand. " And I did. I totally got that he needed to not get tangled up with me and lose his job or his chance at a medal.

But a deep, secret part of me wanted him to chuck it all to be with me. Which, of course, was ridiculous. And if he said he was going to, I wouldn't have let him anyway.

"I should go," I managed to say.

He nodded. "If things were different," he said, looking down at my mouth while gliding his thumb across my bottom lip.

"Don't," I said, my voice no more than a whisper. "You're making it worse."

He took his hand away and squared his shoulders, exhaling loudly. "I'm sorry. I'll see you at practice tomorrow."

Glad he'd put his coach hat back on, I nodded and stepped past him toward the aquatics center.

I only got two steps away before he said, "But Brooklyn?"

Not turning back, I stopped and waited.

"I *was* going to kiss you this morning. I just want you to know that."

Which just made it a thousand times worse.

The Set Up

I returned to Kaylee with the duct tape.

"What's wrong?" she asked right away.

Sure I was going to cry if I opened my mouth, I just shook my head.

"Are you okay?"

All I could do was nod. And anyway, it only sort of felt like a lie if I didn't say it out loud.

"Let's get this done and then you can tell me," she said. I didn't argue, but held the phone while she coiled the tape around it and the tree branch. "This had better work," she muttered. "And I swear, if I get poison oak or something, I'm going to kill Emmie."

I snickered.

She glanced over at me. "That's better. You ready to talk?"

"Not yet. Tell me about Declan. How was dancing with him?"

She ripped the tape with her teeth and secured the end around the phone. "It was good. He's super-cute, right?"

"Way super-cute," I agreed, taking the roll of tape from her, slipping it over my wrist. "And that accent. What is it about guys with accents?"

She turned the camera on and tested the angle, adjusting it slightly. "I don't know. It's so sexy, though. And he's nice, too."

"Unlike Phillip."

She glanced at me and then back to the phone. "Exactly. I'm not sure what I even saw in him."

Well, he is pretty hot, I didn't say, not wanting to remind her. Declan was obviously a way better choice.

She took out her phone to text Celia. After a minute she got a confirmation that mine was streaming to the laptop. "Perfect. Let's go."

We left the phone and went into the aquatics center to meet up with the rest of the girls who were inside. There were ten of us in all after Emmie had outlined the whole plan and we'd spread the word: eight of the original fourteen who'd had their panties stolen and two other girls who'd bought in.

It was almost 10:00 and the boys said to meet them at 10:45, so we had some time. We just had to sit tight and wait, which was maybe the hardest part of this plan.

"So are you excited to see him tonight?" I asked her. It was only us as we walked down the quiet hallway to the locker rooms.

"Yes. And nervous." She gave me a pained look. "He has my underwear."

I smirked at her. "You have his. It's fate."

She rolled her eyes. "Whatever. It's still embarrassing."

"Not as embarrassing as his tightie whities."

"Ha! I think they're cute. I bet he has a nice bum in them."

I laughed. We were about halfway to the locker room when I said, "So. I ran into Brady."

She stopped walking and looked down the hall toward the locker rooms, but we were alone. "What happened?"

I leaned against the wall. "He said he's into me, but he can't jeopardize his job." I couldn't bring myself to give her the particulars, especially about the almost kiss, which I'd been right about in the first place. It felt too private to share: just between him and me.

"That sucks, Brooklyn. I'm sorry."

I shrugged. "It's okay. I knew it wasn't going to work, I guess. I wasn't even sure I really liked him that much." Which felt like a lie, but it was best if she believed it. Even better if I convinced myself, too.

"What about Abe? You seemed to have a good time with him last night."

And then again today, I didn't say. But she was right. He was funny and we seemed to get along really well. Not that I was sure he was even interested *that way,* but he was definitely fun to

156

hang out with.

"Yeah," I said. "He's pretty nice."

"Are you going to go for it?"

I started walking again. "Let's get through this evening first. Come on, we'd better get down the hall or Emmie's going to freak out."

~♥~

The boys were early, though none of us were surprised. We figured they'd come in advance to set up or get in position or whatever it was they needed to do.

So we sat in the locker room of the aquatics center, huddled around Celia's laptop, watching as they muddled around under the outside security lights.

"What are they doing?" Naomi asked.

"Who knows," Chelly said. "Being boys."

And then they disappeared into the bushes. Maybe they thought they would jump out and scare us or something. The camera was aimed at the building, so once they moved into the woods, we couldn't see anything. Celia looked out one of the small windows but said she couldn't see anything other than a few flashes of light. Maybe they were using their phones as flashlights, she said.

At 10:50 (Emmie said we needed to make them sweat a bit and think maybe we weren't coming) we left the locker room and made our way quietly down the hallway to the back door. We were all excited and nervous and I bet every one of our hearts was racing like crazy. I know mine was. We held hands, all ten of us, and walked single file in our Rosewood kilts and blazers.

We stopped at the door to the outside. "Ready, girls?" Emmie asked in a whisper.

"Yes," we all said as one.

And then we made our big entrance.

157

The Big Finale

When we all got outside, we lined up against the back wall of the aquatics center. It was a bit chilly out there in our kilts, but I don't think any of us were too concerned about the temperature. The heat from our excitement was sure to keep us warm.

It smelled a bit like smoke and I hoped the woods weren't on fire or something, but before I had a chance to really think about it, Emmie started the show.

"Boys?" she said, authoritatively, but not too loudly. She knew they were watching. "We're here for our underwear, but we have something for you first. Show yourselves, we're not here to talk to the wood nymphs."

There was a pause and then the bushes started moving and rustling as they moved forward out of the woods. They were all there: Dave, Jenks, Jared, Declan, Phillip, and the rest of the panty-raiders, most of whom I hadn't yet met.

Dave came forward toward Emmie, but she held up her palm to him. "Stay where you are." He gave her a wide-eyed look, but stopped in his tracks.

The guys all looked confused, their eyes darting around from Emmie to us behind her. But none of them said anything, waiting for Emmie's next move. We all were.

I looked at Jared and straightened when I realized he was looking at me. His eyes slid down to my skirt and then back up to my face, questioning me. I blushed, thankful that the security lights were not right on me, so maybe he wouldn't notice. But in response, I tipped my head and shrugged in what I hoped was a coy, *"Maybe I am, maybe I'm not,"* gesture.

He lifted his hand and placed it over his heart.

I smiled, feeling suddenly very powerful.

But then Emmie began in earnest. "So while we came to your campus last night to have some innocent fun at the dance, you snuck over here, violated our rooms and stole our underwear. While I must commend your efforts, despite it being a bit old-school and childish, we Rosewood girls decided to take your little prank, finesse it and give it that extra something."

The guys exchanged glances and it was obvious they had no idea what she was talking about. Kaylee squeezed my hand; she was loving this, too.

"Em, what did you do?" Dave asked.

She seemed to ignore him and continued. "The Rosewood school motto is *alis grave nil*—nothing is too heavy for those who have wings."

She crossed her arms over her chest. "Yes. We stole your underwear. But..." she paused, letting it sink in. And the looks of shock on the boys' faces said everything—this was news to them.

"But, we did more than that. We created a little website and auctioned them off, making over twelve-hundred dollars in just a few hours. All the proceeds going to the charity of our choice, of course."

You could have heard a pin drop in the silence.

"You sold our underwear?" Phillip asked.

"Well, not *yours*," Emmie said, giving him a look. "Funny how no one was interested."

Kaylee chuckled under her breath.

"But, yes," Emmie said, and smug had never looked so good. "For charity."

"To who?" Jenks asked. "Who would buy our underwear?"

"That's the real question, isn't it? Girls?"

And that's when, as one, we turned and lifted our skirts, showing them what, on that day at least, Rosewood girls wore under their kilts.

Epilogue

Once the guys stopped hooting and laughing about us wearing their underwear, they let us in on their original plan, which was to give us our panties back while treating us to a campfire and s'mores. Of course, this was pretty much what Emmie figured they had planned—just another opportunity to hang out with us. Despite not being quite as clever as Emmie's plot, their idea was still pretty nice, so we all headed through the woods to the small campfire they'd built. They'd even pulled logs around for us to sit on.

Jared sat next to me, straddling the log so he faced me on my right side. I was almost completely surrounded by his big body. He was so close, it made my heart skip.

"So, I guess I should give these back to you," he said. I looked down and he was holding my pink underwear. It seemed odd that they were folded neatly. I suppose I was just glad he wasn't holding them up like a trophy.

I shrugged, hiding my awkwardness over him having my panties. I'd barely even been kissed by a guy and this guy was holding my most intimate piece of clothing. "You can keep them, if you want," I said.

He shook his head. "That's creepy. Like, old guy in a trench coat creepy. I'm not that guy. Don't make me into that guy. Please, just take them."

"Okay," I said, laughing as I took the panties from him and stuffed them into my blazer pocket. "But you're getting yours back, too."

He looked surprised. "I thought someone bought them. Doesn't that mean they get to keep them?"

"*Someone* did, but it was a token thing. She doesn't actually *want* them. She doesn't want to be *that* girl." And anyway, *she'd rather see them* on *you*, I didn't say. I shimmied out of his boxer-briefs and handed them to him. He shoved them into his back pocket.

"So," he said, grinning. "How much were they worth?"

I shrugged, playing coy. Also, I didn't really want to tell him. It had sounded great when Emmie'd announced how much we'd made off the auction, but what she *didn't* say was that her opening (and winning) bid for Dave's leopard-print bikinis had been a thousand dollars, thanks to her *Gucci to Goats* program.

"Brooklyn, come on."

"Let's just say the person who bought them was very motivated."

"That's good for the ego," he said.

Speaking of ego, something nagged at me. The old Brooklyn would have let it go, but the new one wanted to know. "Tell me something," I said.

"Mmhmm?"

"Did you end up with mine by accident?"

He dropped his eyes to his hands as he fidgeted his fingers. But I could still see the smile on his face; he was suddenly shy. Which felt weird for a guy who'd lived his life on TV and in the tabloids.

"Jared?"

He was quiet for a moment and I started to think he hadn't heard me. "I like that you call me by my first name," he finally said, still not looking at me. And then his knee nudged mine, the gentle pressure of him touching me feeling like more than just an accidental bump. "I like the way you say it with that hint of an accent."

I didn't say anything, waiting for him to answer, fearing that he was stalling because I was his booby prize.

A long moment passed and I began to fidget, thinking maybe I'd read him wrong.

But then he spoke. "No. It wasn't an accident," he said, finally looking up at me, his emerald green eyes finding mine and holding them, hypnotizing me. "I wasn't the one to take them from your room, but when I saw you at the dance…"

My heart did a little jump then. My lips parted as my lungs suddenly required more air.

He edged closer, his knee pressing into mine. "And then I danced with you and you made me laugh." He grinned. "I'm a sucker for a funny girl."

I'd never been called a funny girl before, but something about being the new Brooklyn made me feel brave and fun. And obviously whatever it was, it was working.

"So I'm just a clown to you, then?" I looked around. "Where's that rainbow wig?"

He grabbed my hand, dwarfing it in his, and tugged me toward him so our foreheads touched. "You're not *just* a clown; you are the *best goddamn looking* clown, who can rock a pair of boxer-briefs like nobody's business."

The new Brooklyn threw back her head and laughed.

Jared rubbed my palm with his thumb and opened his mouth to say something more, but was interrupted by Emmie who suddenly stood up on the other side of the campfire circle. "Everyone, it's getting kind of late and I think we need to shut this party down soon," she paused as everyone booed and groaned. "I know, I know, but we need to put out this fire and get out of here before we attract the attention of security. But before we do, I just want to give a shout out to the newest addition to The Rosewood Academy for Academic Excellence."

I gasped and glanced over at Jared as he squeezed my fingers.

I looked back at Emmie; her eyes were on me.

"Brooklyn, we've only just met you, but already you've proven yourself to be a great roommate and an even greater friend. You didn't even flinch when called to your initiation earlier today."

What?

She smirked. "You didn't even know that was your initiation, did you?"

I shook my head.

"Well you passed, with flying colors. You are definitely a

Rosewood, through and through." As cheers went up around the circle, she looked around. "Don't we have anything to toast her with? God, you boys are so unprepared."

"Toast her with a marshmallow," Dave said.

Emmie rolled her eyes. "Fine." She took the loaded stick Dave offered and set the marshmallow on fire, holding it up over her head like a torch. "To Brooklyn."

Everyone else held their underwear over their head, which made me laugh, but was still kind of fitting. "Hear, hear," they all said. "To Brooklyn."

Jared pulled me into a hug, but over his shoulder, I saw all my new friends smiling and cheering me on.

And just like that, I officially became one of The Rosewoods.

Thank you for reading **TAKING THE REINS!**

I hope you enjoyed it!

Reviews help other readers find books they might enjoy, so I hope you'll consider reviewing this book at retail sites and Goodreads. I appreciate all reviews—positive *and* negative, short and long. Thank you for taking the time to let people know how you felt about this book. This is the best way you can show your love to authors and help them keep writing stories.

The Complete Rosewoods Series

FRESH START (digital exclusive series prequel)

TAKING THE REINS

MASQUERADE

PLAYING THE PART

READING BETWEEN THE LINES

I'LL NEVER FORGET (digital exclusive short story)

THIS POINT FORWARD

RISKING IT ALL (digital exclusive short story)

MAKING RIPPLES

ACTING OUT

HITTING THE TARGET

TURNING THE PAGE

CROSSING THE LINE

If you'd like to keep up to date on new releases, please sign up for my newsletter at: http://eepurl.com/NljKX

Find me online at http://katrinaabbott.com, follow me on Twitter @abbottkatrina and come check out my Pinterest board at https://www.pinterest.com/abbottkatrina/ to see some of the inspirations behind the characters (girls and guys!) and the costumes for MASQUERADE.

xoxo

Katrina Abbott

Out Now!

Masquerade

Book 2

of

The Rosewoods

Turn the page for an excerpt.

One Bad Apple

I glanced at the clock; Dave was late. It was our first meeting as school liaisons and we had plenty to go over, but so far I was on my own.

Not that I was surprised, since it had been five days since Emmie had seen him when the guys had snuck onto our campus, but my nerves were already raw. Every minute I sat there in the study room of the Somerville Library, waiting for Willmont Davidson, or *Dave*, as I now knew him, my dread over seeing him ratcheted up another notch. Or ten.

And it's not because I didn't like him. Quite the opposite. You see, Dave is the first guy I met when I arrived here at The Rosewood Academy for Academic Excellence just a few weeks ago. He's also the first guy I got a huge crush on. *And* it turned out he just happens to be the boyfriend of my roommate, Emmeline Somerville.

Somerville. Yes, the library I was in was named after her family who'd donated it to this very posh and exclusive boarding school. And the reason I was sitting there by myself, in *her* library, was because she and Dave were off making out somewhere, even though he was supposed to be meeting with me. I think that qualifies as some kind of irony.

Letting out a sigh, I returned to my doodling. With Emmie's help earlier (she'd handed over the job of the school liaison to me), I'd made a list of things Dave and I needed to discuss about our joint school events. And there were a lot of events, way more than I'd realized when I'd taken on this job.

The next dance, the Thanksgiving food drive, the Santa Hop and toy drive, and the inter-school mini Olympics. Not to mention the dances that took place next term—it seemed that, to keep the natives happy about Rosewood being an all-girls school, they compensated by having a joint dance with the Westwood boys at least once a month.

I appreciated that as much as the next girl but I had a feeling I was going to need all the help I could get in planning, especially from Emmie who was just about the world's best planner. But if she was going to constantly take off with my school liaison counterpart, this was not going to work.

Finishing up my Jack-O-Lantern doodle beside where I'd written Halloween Dance and a bunch of ideas to go with it, I looked up at the big ticking clock on the wall: almost eight o'clock. Not even counting the fifteen minutes I'd come early, I'd been waiting almost an hour.

Maybe he really isn't coming, I thought. But just then the door opened and the two of them came rushing in. That they were laughing sort of grated on my nerves.

I was a bit angry and disappointed, but I held my tongue—I was still the new girl here and didn't want to make waves. And, even if it didn't seem like it on the outside, I was still feeling weird about having danced with Dave last weekend. Emmie seemed to be over finding out I'd gotten a crush on her boyfriend when I'd first met him (like Kaylee had said, he was just about the hottest guy at Westwood, so who could blame me?), but it still felt awkward, if only in my head.

And no one wants to be the bitchy girl, either. Plus, if I was being honest with myself, if I'd had a boyfriend I'd rather spend time kissing him in the library stacks than let him go to a boring party planning meeting.

I glanced at Dave and then quickly back at the clock, because I had to look *somewhere*. I couldn't focus on him, no matter how good he looked. Actually, the better he looked, the *more* I shouldn't look at him, deathly afraid I was going to get some sort of swoony teenager look stuck on my face that Emmie was going to notice.

"Brooklyn!" she exclaimed, dropping Dave's hand and pulling me up and out of my chair into one of her signature hugs. "I'm so sorry we're late and left you sitting here waiting so long. I promise we have a good excuse."

The two of them had matching pairs of swollen lips, so kissing had definitely been involved, but still I looked at her,

2

waiting for her excuse. I'd only known her for a few weeks, but one thing I knew about my roommate for sure: she was full of surprises. I was almost looking forward to her story.

But then as I dropped back into my chair and she stood there, staring at me, her smile dissolved and then she rolled her eyes. "Okay, we actually don't have a good excuse, but we did bring you a hot chocolate!"

As she said it, Dave was sliding a to-go cup across the table. He smiled and pulled out the chair across from me to sit down.

"Forgive us?" Emmie pleaded.

I nodded toward the cup. "Whipped cream?"

She pressed her hand dramatically over her heart. "Of course, Brooklyn! We're not animals."

I giggled. It was near impossible to stay mad at Emmie. I nodded toward the chair next to her boyfriend, hoping she'd stick around to help.

Dave craned his neck to look at my notebook. "What have you got there?"

"Just the list of all the events."

He reached across the table and grabbed the notebook with a couple of fingers, turning it toward himself.

After a moment, he exhaled. "This is a lot of work."

The way he said it made me think he didn't realize what he'd signed up for. It made me wonder if he'd only signed up because of Emmie. A pang of guilt washed over me. Emmie had traded assignments with me so I could be on the equestrian team; she was now stuck doing laundry in the mornings while I went to equestrian practice and also got to meet with her boyfriend at least once a week, more if we were close to an event.

"I can do most of it," I blurted out, feeling like I owed her, and by extension, him.

Dave looked up at me, frowning. "We're a team. We work together. But I guess we should start with the October dance, since that's the first one."

That made sense. "So should we talk about decorations and Halloween-themed food? Do you know what you're going to

3

dress up as?"

I thought about the dance last weekend—it had been in the gym of the boys' school and all they'd put up were posters of our school crests. I realized the committee didn't have a lot of notice to get ready since school had just started, but it still felt like a pretty weak attempt. Of course, that meant it would be easier for me (and Dave) to pull off something really amazing.

Since the schools alternated, the October dance would be here on the Rosewood campus, making it that much easier to plan. And I had lots of great decorating and snack ideas that I'd found on Pinterest: eyeballs in the punchbowl, ladyfingers that looked like actual fingers, cobweb cupcakes.

Emmie looked at me blankly and then shook her head. "I keep forgetting you're new."

"What does that have to do with anything?"

She glanced at Dave and then at me. "No costumes."

"What?" I looked to Dave for confirmation; he was nodding.

"For a couple of years now," Emmie said. "There was an issue with a few too many slutty costumes, you know: naughty nurse, slutty cop, naughty librarian. I think what threw the dean over the edge was the slutty nun. Someone posted some pictures online and a pissed-off parent freaked out about her daughter going to some sacrilegious dance." She rolled her eyes. "It's ridiculous, but we're not allowed to do costumes anymore."

A Halloween dance with no costumes? "But you called it a Halloween dance. When you said you told your mother to send gowns."

She shrugged. "Because it's at Halloween time. But didn't it strike you as odd that I asked for gowns and not costumes?"

"I thought you were telling her you were going to be an actress or a princess or something."

Emmie just shook her head, giving me a sad look.

"Well that sucks," I said, feeling suddenly deflated.

"No kidding," Dave said.

Emmie smacked his arm half-heartedly. "You just miss all the slutty costumes."

"I think I can speak for all Westwood students," he began in a very huffy voice. "When I say that we miss women being represented in fine professions like nursing, policing and the library sciences. Please, Emmeline. I am a feminist."

I had to give him credit, his face was absolutely deadpan when he said it.

"Right," she said, rolling her eyes. "What about the nuns?"

He grimaced. "I can't support a job that relies so heavily on virtue."

Emmie smacked him again, but I caught her blush. I knew she and Dave hadn't gone all the way yet, although she did tell me that *he* wasn't a virgin. She still was, though. At least, *mostly*, she'd said that night when she'd confided in me. I had no idea what 'mostly' meant, and I didn't dare ask her. We didn't quite know each other that well yet.

"So we can't dress up at all?" I said, trying to break the sudden awkwardness in the room.

She and Dave both shook their heads.

"So what's the point of even having a Halloween dance?"

"It's an *October* dance, not a *Halloween* dance." She said and then her eyes widened. "Don't even think of getting it canceled."

Not that I ever would; with Rosewood being an all-girls' school, our opportunities to hang out with the Westwood boys were few and far between. I was well aware that if I even mentioned the idea of canceling the dance in public, I'd probably be stoned out on the front lawn of the school.

"No, of course not. It just seems pointless to make it a Halloween dance."

"You can still probably do your themed food and stuff," Emmie said, yawning.

That would seem stupid. I wanted to do something special, fun. Memorable. "We have to come up with something." I looked to her for suggestions.

"Well, good luck with that," Emmie said, suddenly standing up. "You know what? I'm bagged, I'm going to bed."

I swallowed and tried to give her a casual look when I said, "Are you sure you don't want to stay and help? I'm sure you have lots of great ideas."

"Nope, I have no ideas. My brain is fried; you two are on your own. I must have loaded eight thousand pounds of sheets this morning. This laundry maid needs her sleep." It was funny that Emmie, maybe one of the wealthiest kids here at Rosewood, did laundry in the bowels of the building every morning. The weirdest part was that she didn't even seem to mind.

She gave me a smile and then turned toward Dave, who stood up to say goodbye to her.

I slid my notebook back across the desk for something to do while she threw her arms around him. Steeling myself to hear *way* too much and wishing it wasn't too awkward to cover up my ears and sing a couple bars of Happy Birthday to drown it out, I drew big loopy circles in the margin of my book, concentrating on my breathing.

He muttered something at her and she responded with loudly and, I'm sure, completely for my benefit: "No tongue, Dave. You know how I feel about juicy PDAs. And anyway, I don't need Brooklyn critiquing my kissing technique."

I smiled, keeping my eyes down on my book, not touching that comment with a ten foot pole.

It was awkward as hell, but no, I couldn't possibly stay mad at Emmie.

Dave returned to the study room after walking Emmie out, closing the door behind him.

I took a sip of the hot chocolate (more like *cold* chocolate by this point) to buy myself a few moments without it being completely awkward. Yeah, that didn't really work.

"So," I said, "I can't believe we aren't allowed to do a costume dance. Is there some other way we can make it fun?"

He dropped into the chair across from me and shrugged. "I don't know. It's too early for Christmas and a Thanksgiving theme isn't really something anyone's going to be interested in. Pilgrim chic isn't really a thing, is it?"

"Sadly, no," I laughed.

"What about some sort of non-holiday theme?"

I exhaled. It was disappointing that the best holiday of the year was going to be kiboshed by school administrators, just because of a few slutty apples.

"There's something special about Halloween," I mused. "Dressing up and being someone else for the night—that's the best part."

"Who do you want to be?" Dave asked quietly.

"Huh?" I looked up at him.

His amazingly blue eyes were boring into mine, looking right inside me. I couldn't look away even if I'd wanted to."If you could dress up and be someone else for the night. Who would you want to be?"

My face heated up and I couldn't look at him anymore, because I was sure he knew I wasn't talking about just wanting to wear a costume. My eyes lowered to my notebook where I resumed doodling. "I don't know. Katniss, maybe."

He was quiet for so long, I had to look up at him again, thinking I'd done something wrong. His head was tilted, curious, and I think he'd been waiting for me to lift my eyes to his before he spoke again. "Why?"

I had an easy out so I took it. "People say I look like her. Jennifer Lawrence, I mean."

Dave sat back in his chair, his eyes moving around my face, taking me in. "You kind of do."

Seeing another opportunity to deflect, I said, "I'm good at archery, too."

He raised an eyebrow. "Is that so?"

I nodded. "My secret talent."

He leaned his chair back onto two legs and gave me a cocky look."Not so secret anymore."

I smiled. "Not if you're going to tell everyone, no, I guess not."

"Maybe I will," he threatened, making me laugh again. "Though I suppose if I did, you'd want revenge and I'd have to watch out for wayward arrows on campus."

"Sir," I said, teasing. "My arrows are *never* wayward."

"Ah," he said, dipping his head in deference. "Touché, ma'am."

Despite the awkwardness (which maybe was only in my head) he really was easy to talk to. He and Emmie made a good couple and even without the fact that he was movie-star good-looking, he was a great catch. He kind of acted like he didn't know how amazing-looking he was, which of course made him that much more attractive.

As I took another sip of my ice-cold chocolate, Dave lifted his arms over his head for a stretch, his Westwood hoodie riding up his body as he reached his fingertips toward the ceiling.

My eyes were drawn to that strip of flesh above his jeans. Something about that narrow line of hair that started at his belly button and disappeared into his pants...

Realizing I needed to totally *not* look there, I lifted my eyes to his. He wasn't smiling anymore, but was watching me oddly. The slight color in his cheeks that hadn't been there a moment before, told me maybe he'd *seen* me looking. And that maybe he thought I was looking even lower than at his stomach.

Nooooooo.

With a sputter, I choked on the liquid in my mouth, spraying it all over the table and my notebook.

And, more than likely, him.

"Oh my God," I said through coughs. "I'm so sorry!" Which just made me choke more. I dissolved into a total hacking fit.

"Are you okay?"

No, I'm not okay, I thought. I kind of wanted to die in that moment. No, I *definitely* wanted to die. *Ugh.*

He got up to come around the table. "Brooklyn? You okay?" he asked again, giving me a sharp smack on the back. And then another as I continued to cough.

I managed to gasp out, "I'm fine." Which wasn't all that convincing.

He must have realized there wasn't anything more he could do because he returned to the other side of the table, but he stood there at attention, waiting.

"You sure? Need me to get you some water or something?"

Holding my hand up, I shook my head, heaved through a few more coughs and prayed for the floor to open up under me.

On the plus side, my tomato-red face could no longer be *just* from embarrassment over getting caught looking at his belly.

After another moment, he sat in his chair; I could feel his eyes trained on me, but I didn't dare look at him.

Finally, when I was mostly back to normal, I reached into my backpack and pulled out some Kleenex. I took a tissue out to wipe my watering eyes and then another to try to clean the hot chocolate off the table.

"You okay?" Dave asked again, suddenly making me *really* want to use him for archery practice.

"Peachy," I said, my voice raspy. I finally forced myself to look at him to see the damage. His navy blue hoodie seemed fine, but then my eyes rose to his face.

God, there was a drop of hot chocolate on his cheek. I handed him a Kleenex. "Sorry. I got you." I pointed at the place on my own face corresponding to his.

"Other side," I said when he tried to get it and completely missed.

He wiped it off and looked at me with raised eyebrows.

"Yeah, you got it," I said. I got up out of my chair and threw out the rest of the hot chocolate and the wet tissues, grabbing his on my way to the wastepaper basket. I somehow managed to fight the urge to just keep walking to the door and right out of the library.

Want more? Get Masquerade at your favorite book retailer today!

Made in the USA
Middletown, DE
07 December 2024